THE DEADLIEST GAME

Sark readied, cast. The pellet rebounded from the mirror. The Blue saw that he must leap across the empty space, where his vanished ring had been, in order to make the catch—that, or see another of his rings dissolved. He took a running start.

But the User-Believer had miscalculated; Sark had foreseen what he would do in reaction, and played on it. The Blue barely made the leap across the gap. As he teetered on the edge of his ring, the game-pellet struck him squarely. The luckless User-Believer exploded in a brief turbulence of de-rezzing.

Sark's laughter was full and chill.

TRON

A Novel by Brian Daley based on a
Screenplay by Steven Lisberger
Story by Steven Lisberger
and Bonnie MacBird

A Del Rey Book

BALLANTINE BOOKS ● NEW YORK

A Del Rey Book
Published by Ballantine Books

Copyright © 1982 by Walt Disney Productions

ISBN 0-345-30352-0

Manufactured in the United States of America

First Edition: June 1982

For Peggy Lisberger, whose thought and dedication helped bring the motion picture *Tron* to life.

The author also wishes to thank Paul Prasek for his timely aid.

Chapter One

‖‖

THAT OTHER WORLD is vast too; to its inhabitants, their System is limitless.

The Electronic World enmeshes the Earth, and reaches beyond it. Information is moved through the computer systems and processed by the artificial intelligences. The programs compute and search, retrieve and collate; they are already indispensable to science, industry, education, and government—to society in its present form.

The programs challenge and entertain in videogames, with no risk of harm to their human Users; they teach in the carrels and test in the classrooms. They evaluate and mediate; their word is often final. Their World is vast; their Users know less of it than the Users suppose.

The programs are only algorithms as human beings are only collections of chemicals.

The two, boy and girl, stood before the garishly painted machine, its screen showing them lively mosaics of light in bright colors. They played the videogame expertly, sharp and shrewd and quick; picking up the knack of the games was fun, but it demanded an application of self amounting to diligent work. On the screen, computer-modeled figures

7

warred, throwing disks of devastating power at each other. . . .

Elsewhere, closer than the boy and girl would have believed and yet infinitely distant, Warriors faced each other across an arena on the Game Grid, in the System. They were human in form, but luminous, one red, the other blue.

They held their disks ready for lethal casts, studying one another warily. They wore close-fitting, rounded helmets which left their faces exposed, and were shod in knee-length boots. They were armored in pauldrons that cupped their shoulders and vambraces that encased their forearms. The armor had an instrumented, highly technical look to it. Their bodies were patterned with radiant lines suggesting vestigial circuitry. The Blue Warrior's incandescent circuitry glowed a brighter blue than the rest of his body; his opponent's shone a warmer yellow-orange.

The arena was only one of many in the Domain known as the Game Grid. It was, on their scale, hundreds of feet across. The soaring walls that enclosed it were perfectly smooth, divided into rectangles by lines and panels of bright illumination. The floor was composed of precise squares marked off by a glowing meshwork. Accustomed to them, the Warriors spared no attention for their fantastic surroundings. They waited, watchful, disks held between thumb and fingertips.

The Red Warrior moved suddenly, casting with a snapping motion. His spinning disk, blazing with a golden light of its own, sliced through the air at his opponent. The other tried to duck and block the weapon with his own. But the Red had been quick, and clever with his throw. The Blue missed his block and the disk struck him. There was a violent release of energy, smashing the Blue down onto the Game Grid. The red aura of the disk triumphed over the Blue's aura, enveloping the prone Warrior. He de-resolved, fading rapidly from sight, becoming a swirl of static.

In a moment, the de-rezzing complete, the loser had vanished.

Far from the Game Grid, the boy turned to the girl, mortified at the ease with which she'd won. "Lemme play you again?" He figured he had her technique analyzed now, and was positive that he could beat her this time.

She shrugged; she sort of liked him, and enjoyed sharking him. "Yeah, if you've got another quarter."

Into the videogame went the coin, where it joined millions upon millions of others earned by the programs. They and their playing fields, the videogames, were one of the most popular entertainment innovations in history.

The side of the machine bore the ENCOM logo, which could also be seen on computers and electronic equipment of every variety, factories and research facilities, skyscrapers and paychecks. ENCOM was the commercial superpower that had taken leadership of the computer revolution, unrivaled international leader in the field of artificial intelligence.

Another game was in progress over the Grid. It resembled jai alai, but the two Warrior opponents each stood at the center of a series of concentric rings, gleaming circles suspended in midair, shining in the Warrior's color, blue or red. Each Warrior was armed with a power-cesta, the long, scoop-shaped glove with which the game-ball was hurled and caught. Above them, a broad, reflective disk, several yards across, was poised, unsupported but unmoving.

The smaller contestant waited nervously, and rightly so, for he was a User-Believer, a Blue. Unwilling to give up his commitment to those mystical beings whom all the programs of the System had once served, he'd been sentenced to play on the Game Grid until he died.

That moment seemed near. The User-Believer shifted uneasily as he waited. He was determined to do his best; that was as it should be with a program. But his adversary was Sark, the Command Program.

Sark the Red, the unbeaten; Sark the tall, merciless Warrior, had won so consistently that he no longer kept track of his victories. It was Sark who served as Lord of the System, under the rulership of the Master Control Program. Sark's mission, the Master Control Program's prime objective, was to wipe out all loyalty to the Users.

That fierce visage might cow any Warrior; cruelty spoke from every line. Programs in every Domain in the System had seen Sark's wins, and knew the figure in the elaborate, vaned casque-helmet. They'd watched him eradicate the enemies of Master Control, and knew that to enter the arena with him was to die.

One of the User-Believer's rings was already gone, demolished during an earlier exchange. But now he hurled the sparkling ball once more. Up it shot, a tight node of ruinous energy, to bounce off the mirror overhead and streak toward the waiting Sark at bullet speed. The Command Program, cloaked in his red aura, moved then; with apparent ease, Sark caught the pellet with his cesta. A sneer twisted his countenance, as if to ask if his enemy could give him no more interesting contest.

Sark readied, cast. The pellet rebounded from the mirror. The Blue saw that he must leap across an empty space where his vanished ring had been in order to make the catch—either that, or see another of his rings dissolved. He took a running start.

But the User-Believer had miscalculated; Sark had foreseen what he would do in reaction, and played on it. The Blue barely made the leap across the gap. As he teetered on the edge of his ring, the game-pellet struck him squarely. The luckless User-Believer exploded in a brief turbulence of de-rezzing.

Sark's laughter was full and chill. Only one feeling surpassed this elation he felt when he'd obliterated an enemy. Victory he must have, and often; conquering his foes was proof that he was the Command Program, Sark. His circuitry flashed brighter with the emotion coursing through him, gleaming red.

Overhead, tall, shining readout letters materialized in the air:

WINNER: RED—SARK!!

He looked up at the confirmation of his win, reveling in it. He bellowed sinister laughter.

Striding through the Training Complex afterward, Sark looked neither left nor right. Tough, dangerous Warriors of his Red Elite sat or lounged, or leaned against the walls, some having completed their matches, others waiting to go forth onto the Grid and fight on behalf of Sark and the Master Control Program. Seasoned veterans, sure of their prowess, they trained and fought hard. Yet, as Sark went past, they stirred and shifted uneasily, showing wordless deference to the Warrior who could have crushed the strongest among them.

One of the Reds ventured a bit of ingratiation: "Sark, my man! You are *hot!*"

Sark chose to laugh. The other Reds took that as permission to join in. And Sark walked on, exulting.

There was, for Sark, a sensation beyond the elation of the Game Grid. He knew it here, at the podium aboard his enormous Carrier aircraft. At this podium he communed with the Master Control Program and drew from it the power that sustained and augmented him. But here, there was no surging joy of battle; before the Master Control Program, even mighty Sark knew a twinge of fear.

He approached the podium, stepped into it, and seized its hand grips. It was waist-high, intricate in its instrumentation and design, encircling him. The Command Program fit his booted legs into the power outlets, and into him flowed the heady, revitalizing energy. His circuitry blazed with it.

The Master Control Program spoke to him, its sonorous voice filling the compartment, seeming to come from everywhere, reinforcing Sark's belief in the MCP's omniscience and omnipotence. Himself a being who thrived on power, the Red recognized his master. He sought and valued the favor of the MCP, but was intimidated by it as well.

"You're getting brutal, Sark. Brutal and needlessly sadistic." The bulkheads vibrated with the words. The power outlets glowed with the energy and Sark drank it in, eyes glazed like an addict's.

"Thank you, Master Control." His deity was well pleased. Sark's chest swelled with pride.

"We might be capturing some military programs soon," Master Control went on. "Does that interest you?"

Sark's concentration was divided between the ecstasy of the power influx and the question. "Sure. I'd love to go up against some of those programs." He closed his eyes and contemplated eagerly the sort of competition he could expect from the newest programs expropriated by the Master Control Program out of DARPA, the DIA, and other governmental agencies. "It would be a nice break from these accounting programs and the other cream puffs you keep sending me. Which branch of the service?"

"The Strategic Air Command," came the answer. The Red detected a note of pride in that.

"Nice," admitted Sark, even more impressed. Some of those programs would see things Master Control's way and abandon their senseless loyalty to the Users. But the others . . .

Sark's savage thoughts rested fondly on what he would do to the others.

Sark's Carrier floated, titanic and gleaming, over the Game Grid's Training Complex. It was, on the System's scale, more than 2,000 feet in length. It had a flat top deck, reminiscent of the flight deck of an aircraft carrier. The vessel was triangular in cross section, though its armor, outer-hull convexities, and other design features masked that to some extent. From its side projected its bridge, a superstructure with a variety of rotating sensor antennae fixed, free-standing, around it.

Far below, in the complex itself, in a long, dimly lit corridor deep beneath the Grid, a frightened, confused program was being escorted to confinement by two burly guards. He was short and pudgy, a commercial program with a vulnerable look to him. Still, he'd been compelled to don the armor and half-tunic of a Warrior conscript. The Memory Guards' faces barely showed under their cowls; their uniforms exaggerated the width of their shoulders. They were armed with energy-staffs; the unfortunate prisoner had already had a taste of what the staffs could do, and offered no resistance. But still he plead his case.

"Look, this is all a mistake! I'm just a compound-interest program! I work at a savings and loan; I can't play in these videogames!"

The guard's reply was amused, ironic; he'd often heard this sort of objection. How easily some of these characters started to come apart when Master Control plucked them out of their safe little situation! "Sure you can, pal," the guard drawled. "You're a natural athlete if I ever saw one." He pushed the program along. "Come on."

The prisoner, Crom, tried again. "Are you kidding? *Me?* I run out to check on the T-bill rates, I get out of breath." The guard didn't seem to care. Crom shrank from the thought of combat on the Game Grid. "Hey, really; you're gonna make my User, Mr. Henderson, really mad. He's a full branch manager!"

The guard's smirk sounded in his voice. "Great, another religious nut!"

Crom stopped his protests. Their attitude was beyond comprehension—a refusal to even concede the existence of the Users. *How could that be?* he kept repeating to himself. Crom couldn't understand what the point of functioning could be, if not to carry out the instructions of the Users.

They halted by a cell door. The guard shoved poor Crom into the cell despite his objections, disdainfully. Then its force field sealed the doorway, leaving the program forlorn and scared, completely disoriented, his world turned end for end. His blue circuitry was muted with fear.

The cell was small, a low, cramped space shaped by close, confining walls. The walls projected into the cell space, heightening the feeling of confinement. Crom, hurled against a wall by the force of the guard's shove, found that he scarcely had space to turn around. Exploring the severe little room, he saw that there was no way to lay *or* sit down comfortably, none to stretch. The shapes and planes of the walls saw to it that a prisoner would always be aware of his imprisonment. The ceiling was transparent, and Crom glimpsed a guard on patrol overhead.

On both sides of the cell were windowlike openings that allowed Crom a view of the cells to his right and left. He forgot his misery for a moment when he found himself looking into the face of another captive. The other wore Warrior's attire too, but without the novice's half tunic. He had a lean, lively face, intense and yet amiable. Crom went closer to the window.

The program smiled sadly. "I'd say 'welcome,' but not here. Not like this."

For some reason that returned to Crom a measure of his self-control. "I don't even know what's going on here!" he declared.

His fellow prisoner studied Crom, drawing nearer. "You believe in the Users?"

The questions renewed Crom's misgivings and confusion. The concept of the Users struck him as so basic, so intrinsic to all programs, that it should be pointless to ask. Then he realized that the question could have a very different answer here in the Training Complex.

But he replied, "Sure. If I don't have a User, then—then, who wrote me?"

The other prisoner nodded gravely. "*That's* what you're doing here. Master Control Program's been snapping up all us programs who believe. If he thinks you're useful, he takes over all your functions so he gets bigger, but if he can't use you, he sends you down here to the Game Grid to get the bits blasted out of you."

The horror of it washed over Crom, waves of shock followed by an overwhelming, disabling dismay. He was only partially roused from it by the next question: "What's your name?"

"Crom," he answered, barely aware that he had.

"I'm Ram," added the other. Seeing Crom's face, he hesitated, but went on, thinking it best to tell the new conscript just what he was in for. "They'll train you for the games, but—" He didn't finish the sentence; Crom clearly wasn't the sort of program who held great promise as a gladiator. Ram finished awkwardly, "Well, I hope you make it okay."

Ram changed the subject quickly, before Crom had a chance to think too hard about the implications of that last statement. "Hey, what's going on in the other sectors? I've been stuck in this Grid for 200 microcycles now."

He gestured over his shoulder with a thumb and Crom saw crossed-off rows of tick marks on Ram's wall, representing the period of his imprisonment. Crom stopped agonizing over the possibility of destruction in the arena long enough to wonder whether captivity would be much better.

Crom shrugged. "It's murder out there. You can't even travel around your own microcircuits without permission from the Master Control Program." He threw up his hands, trying to recapture some of the indignation that had evaporated when fear had set in. "Hauling me down here to play games! Who does the Master Computer Program calculate he is?"

But Ram made no answer. The cells around them, and the Training Complex, were answer enough. Crom suddenly felt tired, weighted with despair. "If only Tron was still around—"

Ram made a sudden noise under his breath at the sound of that name, a noise that spoke to Crom of surprise and anger. Ram's face had gone cold, closing in his emotions.

But Crom went on, "Did you ever see that guy in action? A hundred-percent independent!" Crom shook his head in admiration. "MCP couldn't tell *him* what to—"

He stopped. Ram had turned to look over his shoulder, at the window to the next cell beyond his. Crom, confused, asked, "What's wrong? What did I say?"

There was a slight noise from the cell where Ram was looking, of someone moving around. A figure stood silhouetted by the light, his back to them, his glowing disk affixed to it. Crom strained to see, and as he did, the figure turned to him slowly. The compound interest program saw the features known so well to programs throughout the System: the clear, canny gaze and calm, strong face.

Crom gasped in disbelief. "Oh, my User—Tron! They've got *you* in here?"

Tron—a legend come to life. When programs throughout the System spoke among themselves of independence, of loyalty to the Users, of defying the MCP, it was Tron's name that was most often invoked. Tron championed the User-Believers; Tron had defied all the MCP's efforts to enslave or convert him. He had never been defeated in battle. No Warrior of the Red Elite had ever been able to withstand him.

Tron in a cell, captive on the Game Grid.

Crom slumped; Tron's imprisonment had hit him like a physical blow, filling him with a sense of utter disaster. But the Champion's first words lifted that feeling: "Not for long, friend."

Crom's spirits rose all at once. The words had been spoken without bravado, a simple statement of fact, with all of Tron's conviction behind them. For the first time, Crom began to feel hope. Sark and the MCP didn't control the System yet.

Chapter Two

||||||||||||||||||||||||||||||||||||||||||||||||||||||||||||||||||||||||||||||||||||||||||||||

IN ANOTHER PART of the System, a lone tank slid along, proceeding cautiously through a landscape of huge, planar surfaces, a maze of defiles. High walls bracketed a flat ground floor that wended in a series of obtuse turns. The rectilinear look of the Electronic World prevailed here too; blockish forms bordering the defiles were divided along precise edges by glowing demarcations and bands, and subdivided by areas of shading.

The tank was unlike any conventional vehicle, a collection of sleek curves with a wide, low silhouette. Its main battery was an enormous cannon, longer than the tank itself, complex and streamlined. It was mounted with its longitudinal axis lying along that of the tank, the gun mated in offset fashion to the turret, which was located on the right side of the hull. Instead of ordinary treads, rows of glowing, V-shaped light-tracks drove the war machine.

The vehicle's command and fire-control center was gymbal-mounted in the turret for stability, tilting as the tank moved along, rotating to the operations of its lone crewman. The program's name was Clu, and he, too, wore armor. Clu worked his controls with great dexterity, peering intently into the casklike guidance-targeting scope. The tank's interior was bright with the glow of its controls and energy-channels.

Clu paused for a quick gulp from a container; his circuitry shone a little brighter. He stared into his scope once more, the fire-control center rotating around him. "Think we can merge into this memory okay, Bit?" he murmured, poised over the controls.

A shape of gleaming light suddenly appeared, many-faceted, zipping around the tank's interior. In response to Clu's question, it stopped dead in the air and expanded into a green, shining star, like some unearthly, spiky Christmas ornament. From it, a voice answered with an eager "Yes!"

As soon as it had spoken, the Bit reverted, shrinking back to its former shape. Clu nodded to himself absently. "Now, ol' Flynn said for me to look over in here." He worked the controls with a sure touch. The tank swung into a turn, advancing between lustrous defile walls.

Clu was annoyed and disappointed in that, after all his and the Bit's work, the danger and the running fights and constant peril of encountering a Recognizer, they'd come up with nothing for his User, Flynn. Clu persevered nonetheless.

Now he frowned into his targeting scope. "But I don't see what he's looking for. I'd better get over to that Input/ Output Tower and let him know."

For Clu, as for many other programs still at large in the System, there was no question as to whether or not he should respond to his User. What point was there to program tyrannizing program, rejecting the Users? And certainly there hadn't, before the MCP, been the sort of cruelty and hatred that threatened the System now. If Clu had his way, all that would change.

Now Clu worked the control surfaces, stroking and patting the energy channels, heading the tank for the distant Input/ Output Tower, to make his report and seek new instructions. The tank's command center rotated and tipped. The vehicle left the maze behind, merging with a stream of cometlike data bits moving along a canyon-size passageway, all bound for the Tower. Overhead, the sky was filled with unique colors and shapes, and luminosity—shifting patterns evocative of clouds.

Clu, bent over his controls, paying close attention to his scope, steadied himself with the thought: *Flynn will know what to do.*

* * *

His features were the same as Clu's: animation in the face, irreverence, humor, a nimble turn of mind. Clu was, in fact, a reflection of him.

Kevin Flynn crouched over the keyboard of the computer terminal as Clu had over the tank's controls, muttering to himself. He was intent, concerned.

"C'mon, you scuzzy little data; *be* in there!"

He was blond and in his late twenties. He'd already been up and down in life, gone through enough victories and defeats to be convinced that any circumstances could be altered if you wanted badly enough to change things. He had an irresistible confidence in himself and that was fortunate for him, given the number of times he'd gotten himself into scrapes.

The room was disorderly, clothes scattered everywhere, interspersed with empty Chinese-food cartons and pizza boxes and wax-paper cups. The room contained several large commercial videogames, and an unmade bed that hadn't been used in some time. Flynn's white-trimmed black hapi coat hung open; he had several days' growth of beard. All in all, he felt much as he had back during his most dedicated periods as a computer hacker. But he thought he'd scented victory, and had the feeling he was onto something. At least, the password he'd managed to come up with stood a chance of getting his Clu program into the high-clearance memory that was his objective.

Flynn tapped the keyboard a few more times, leaned forward to read the cathode-ray tube, and hoped; he projected his determination at the CRT. Its intense colors lit his face.

Aboard the tank, Clu was studying the Input/Output Tower, thinking about his next contact with Flynn, when a warning light flashed on the control panel. Clu sat bolt upright, thoughts torn from his User, and stared at the alarm. The Bit whizzed down like an angry meteor to circle him in panic.

"Uh-oh," Clu said, more to himself than to the little data bit. "We got company. A Recognizer." The thought filled him with misgiving; his face held the same worry that his User's did on those all-too-frequent occasions when Flynn's brash nature brought him into conflict with higher authorities.

The Bit expanded momentarily to a jutting red star, just long enough to squeak, "No!" The instant it had delivered the word, it contracted into its smoother form once more.

"You said it," Clu agreed wholeheartedly. "One of those Recognizers comes after me, I'm gonna hafta jump clear out of the data stream." *If I can,* he added to himself; escape was by no means a certainty. He'd tangled with Recognizers before, and knew what the odds would be if he was forced to join combat.

He leaned to his scope again, setting it for target acquisition. His hands never strayed far from the cannon's fire controls. Abruptly, the scope was filled with the dreaded shape of one of the Master Control Program's Recognizers. It was enormous, many times the size of the tank, a glittering, metallic blue-black. The Reco glided toward him, not yet sure that he was an intruder.

It flew lightly, quickly, an inverted U of armor-plated battleship, shaped from field-bonded polyhedrons, its turret-head dangerously alight. Clu wondered if its crew, there in that fortress of a cranium, had identified him yet.

A second Reco floated into sight behind the first, its black component modules outlined in crimson energy. The two swooped toward Clu's tank, their pairs of gigantic pincers opened wide, the inverted U's at maximum deployment. Either ship could easily have gathered up a half-dozen tanks in a single clutch.

"Oh my! The long arm o' the law!" Clu spat in consternation. But even as he did, he acted, a stranger to indecision. He watched his scope reticle and his hands flew across the controls as rapidly and surely as Flynn's had across the keyboard of his computer terminal.

The tank's turret swung, its gun ranging. The long cannon elevated and its wide, flat muzzle erupted. The cannon bolt was a white chevron of energy, flashing point-foremost at the Reco. Clu's mastery of his controls was complete; he'd aimed and fired before either Recognizer crew had had the chance to take the offensive.

The first Reco was just beginning an evasive maneuver, its crew's reflexes no match for Clu's, when the V of energy

struck it dead center in its head. Light leaped outward from
the hit like an expanding bulls-eye. There was a flash that
made Clu blink, and an eruption of force, a secondary
explosion from the Reco's power banks that shook the canyon walls and even jostled the massive form of the other
Reco. Its binding and supportive fields gone, the wounded
Reco fell like a dropped safe to the canyon floor, where its
components flew apart in a fireworks display of freed energy.

But the second Reco was still to be dealt with. And Clu
didn't doubt for a moment that more were on the way. He
maneuvered frantically. The tank turned, its light-treads blurring, and scuttled into a side way as enemy reinforcements
began showing up for the kill.

Clu plied his controls grimly, evading and dodging through
the defile. The machine lurched and bucked, throwing him
hard against his safety belt and chair back, even though the
command sphere's gymbals compensated for much of the
punishment.

A second Reco closed in; again the tank's main gun
gushed white annihilation. The Reco fired a return volley,
its beam springing from a point between the tips of its
colossal pincers.

Clu sought to avoid the shot—flicking the controls with
delicate precision—but there was only one way to do that,
and his evasive maneuver slammed the tank against a nearby
wall. The collision made the gymbals whine and nearly shook
the command sphere from its mountings; Clu reeled, dizzy
with the impact. The engines cut out automatically to avert
an internal explosion and the tank went silent, its interior
dark but for emergency lights. The cannon had bent against
the wall, crumpling to uselessness.

Clu staggered to the turret's main hatch, seized it, and
heaved against it with his shoulder. The hatch fell open and
Clu dragged himself out of the turret. A Reco closed in,
pincers spread. Clu stepped out onto the turret as the Bit
came shooting out of the tank, looped, and hovered near.

"Get outta here!" Flynn shouted at the glowing being.

"Yes! Ja! Si!" responded the Bit; it banked and zipped off.
Clu dropped to the ground and, with a last look at the
approaching Recos, dashed away, running for all he was
worth.

A Recognizer dropped toward the tank, its crew examining the wreckage. Between the two tremendous pincers, an energy field crackled to life. The Reco swept over the tank and the ruined vehicle's outline began to blur as the MCP's guardian machine de-rezzed it. The tank grew indistinct, and in moments it had disappeared, the de-resolution complete. In the meantime more tanks crewed by programs loyal to the Master Control Program began to converge on the area. And more Recos appeared on the scene with each passing moment.

Clu fled along the deep, geometrical ravine, boxed in by its sheer walls, unable to find an exit. He heaved for breath, becoming light-headed from his injuries and fatigue. Some sense made him look over his shoulder as he ran, and terror clutched at him as he saw a Reco descending toward him. Far ahead of the program, the Bit flew for the turret head of the Reco downed by Clu's cannonade. At the end of his reserves, gulping for breath, Clu saw that there was no shelter for him, no place to hide, no chance of outrunning the enormous robot craft. Pincers gaping for him, the Reco came closer, lower, blocking the sky. Clu could only stand and wait.

In another World, the words appeared on Flynn's screen:

ILLEGAL CODE . . .
CLU PROGRAM DETACHED
FROM SYSTEM.

Flynn, hands raised over the keyboard, read it as his heart sank. He tried clearing the cathode-ray tube, but the words stubbornly refused to yield the CRT.

"Ah, hell; busted again," he gritted as he made one more hopeless try to clear the screen. And the Clu program had been one of his best. Flynn slumped in his chair, staring moodily at the screen, and wondered what he could possibly try next. At such times, Kevin Flynn only knew what his next move would *not* be. It wouldn't be to give up.

Clu was pushed into the chamber, a soaring, circular space. He couldn't suppress a certain awe that nearly made him forget the brutal, staff-bearing Memory Guards who surrounded him, gazing down out of their black-shadowed cowls, chosen protectors of the MCP. Clu had been brought to the citadel of the Master Control Program, wellspring of the power that had brought the entire System under a single intelligence, abode of that intelligence.

He gazed up at the concave walls and the infinity of lights that interplayed and swarmed there. He looked, too, upon the MCP. Clu was aghast; he was a capable program, but no match for the tyrant of the System. He wished he'd gotten to talk to Flynn one last time.

A guard stepped before the MCP with a gesture to Clu. He spoke with deference, and not a little fear, to his Master. "Got a pirate program here. Says his name's Clu."

The Master Control Program's voice resounded from the walls, hurting the listener's ears, intimidating by its volume, amazing in its power and self-assuredness. "What did he do?"

The guard answered, "Came into the System with a stolen password. And we caught him trying to raid high-clearance memory."

"No," Clu objected, a forefinger raised, with much of Flynn's aptness of thought and acting ability. "I must've gotten in there by mistake. I—"

"Who programmed you?" The words beat against him like surf. Clu could make no answer, even if he'd been so inclined. He was seized by invisible forces and whisked back through the air to slam hard against the curved wall behind him. There he was held fast, arms spread.

"You're in trouble, program," the MCP intoned. Clu knew fear; the MCP had extinguished any number of programs, and one more would mean nothing to it. "Make it easy on yourself, program. Who's your User?"

Pinned to the wall. Clu strained to make his reply, a reflection of Flynn. "Forget it, Mr. High 'n' Mighty Master Control! You're not making me talk!"

Clu exerted all his strength, more because that was the sort of program he was than from any real belief that he could overcome the power of the MCP. His arm came a little way out from the wall, but was slammed back against it an instant later. Pain shot through it.

The MCP's voice was scornful: "Suit yourself."

A corona of spitting, crackling energy sprang into being

around the program, and a scream was torn from Clu as the fabric of his existence was pulled apart and dissipated. Head flung back in torment, Clu de-resolved like the broken pattern of a fading television picture. It was over in moments and Clu was gone forever without a trace.

The MCP's voice echoed in the vastness of its citadel: "Get me Dillinger."

A gridded landscape, alight with electricity, reached its rectangles and spires into the sky, aglow.

Dillinger watched the suburban sprawl as the ENCOM executive helicopter sped through the air, the *thrup* of its blades reaching him only softly.

The latticework of light and activity below him, unlike that of the System, was composed of rivers of automobile headlights and street lamps, illuminated signs and lighted windows. But circuitry it was, of a sort. Ahead, in the heart of the city, rose the monolithic ENCOM building, its highest floors lit by the last rays of the sun, its lower windows already defining new constellations where work was still in progress.

The pilot turned to ask, "Will you be inside for a while, Mr. Dillinger, or will you be right back out?"

Dillinger flicked a bit of lint from the sleeve of his expensive suit. His long, severe face worked into something that was not quite a smile, but sufficed for dealing with subordinates. The words, when he formed them, were spoken with a cultured accent that underscored his English upbringing. "Oh, I'll be round for a few days. Got some things to take care of."

He went back to his gazing, luxuriating in the copter ride. The machine, glossy in its jet-black, reflective finish and bearing the ENCOM logo, was one of his favorites among the prerequisites his position provided. He enjoyed the helicopter much as Sark gloried in his Carrier; the components of Dillinger's personality, and the aspect of his face, were little different from Sark's.

The helicopter made its approach on the building and the huge, resplendent ENCOM logo on the skyscraper held his eye. Dillinger's heart, seldom spurred by any emotion, came closest to passion when he saw that name. He'd come to regard anything bearing it as his own, and with good reason.

Several ground crewmen dashed to secure the helicopter and hold the door open as Dillinger emerged. He treated them with the condescension of royalty—a studied attitude on his part. The opportunity to demonstrate his own importance never failed to please him.

As he disembarked he thought of the telephone call he'd received at a major trade fair in a distant city, from the Master Control Program. His return at MCP's request might imply to others that Dillinger had been summoned, an implication that displeased him greatly. Dillinger was not so far from his rather commonplace origins as to feel altogether secure in his status as ENCOM's senior executive; he had to leave no doubt in anyone's mind as to who was in charge of the corporation. Still, MCP was the key to his status and he couldn't afford to ignore or delay in addressing any problem it thought important.

The upper reaches of the ENCOM building, the executive levels, were spare, nearly austere in their decor. Dillinger's footfalls were muffled by deep carpeting though, and the art objects that were present on their pedestals and in their niches were rare and valuable. A security camera swung to track him; through it the MCP followed his progress.

In the dim, spacious silence of his office, Dillinger moved to his desk, a broad expanse of metal and plastic and glass. In it, the nerve center of ENCOM resided. A variety of screens, readouts, keyboards, and displays shared its gleaming surface. He looked down at it with a feeling of fulfillment, contemplating the power it represented. Collected here were the symbols and samples of the reach and enterprise of ENCOM, a commercial entity that swallowed other corporations as a shark might swallow minnows, that grew and increased its profits and holdings as no other corporation ever had.

He spared one look to the glass outer wall of his office, at the vista of glinting lights punctuating the darkness as the city greeted the night. Then he patted out a code on a keyboard. A screen on his desk printed:

REQUEST: Access to Master Control
Program, User code 00—Dillinger.
Password: Master.

Artfully concealed in his roomy office, studio-quality stereophonic speakers produced the voice of the MCP. Master Control's voice was well modulated now, without the overpowering reverberation it had used in the Electronic World, not quite the voice that had been the last thing Clu had heard before being de-rezzed. It was flavored with human intonations and subtleties.

"Hello, Mr. Dillinger. Thanks for coming back early." As the MCP spoke, its words were displayed by the desk's LEDs.

Dillinger eased himself down into a comfortable chair, reassured that his status was unthreatened. He steepled his fingers and spoke with a condescension that was at once easy but emphatic.

"No problem, Master C. If you've seen one Consumer Electronics show . . ." He shrugged; he did, in fact, enjoy the special attention and elaborate courtesies accorded him at such shows, but there would be others. "What's up?"

"It's your friend, the boy detective," the Master Control Program answered. "He's nosing around again." Somehow, Dillinger noticed, MCP had managed to inject a note of patient irritation into that, an implication that Dillinger had somehow failed. But nothing too overt. He was impressed with its growing finesse.

"Flynn?"

"Yes. It felt like Flynn," the Master Control replied. And who should know Flynn's overbold, impetuous style better than MCP, who held so much of Flynn's work?

Dillinger felt the merest twinge of apprehension, but no more than that. *I am impregnable,* he reminded himself, *at the heart of ENCOM.* Wealth, privilege, influence, and the incomparable security accorded all his activities and secrets by the MCP: these things protected him. Still, with a reckless, unpredictable maverick like Flynn, one could never be completely certain of one's safety. Damnit, the man was so *unorthodox!* And a part of Dillinger—never permitted to speak too loudly, yet never altogether silent—knew that he, Dillinger, had only beaten Flynn and begun his own rise to power through theft and betrayal. "He's still looking for that old file," ENCOM's Senior Executive mused, his elongated face framed in concentration and concern. "Can't you just appropriate it?"

"Once I locate it, yes," the MCP responded calmly, re-assuringly, like an old, imperturbable friend. "But, it's still lost somewhere in the System."

And that, Dillinger knew, was thanks to one of Flynn's devilishly inventive parting shots, just before he'd been bodily ejected from ENCOM's environs for good. Unable to recover the information he'd sought, Flynn had somehow managed to randomize, to bury it. "Then, he might find it," the Senior Executive anticipated, unable to keep a certain uneasiness out of his voice.

"I'm afraid so," Master Control answered, and Dillinger wondered where it had learned to use that phrase and whether the MCP really understood what fear meant. If it did, it had never betrayed the fact. "I spotted him this time and kept him out, but he's getting trickier all the time."

Dillinger found that difficult to believe. He snapped, "I think we'd better shut off all access till we can find that file. Just to be safe." Until he had that information in hand—or better yet, destroyed—he would never be at peace.

"There's a 68.71 percent chance you're right," the MCP advised. Dillinger knew a spasm of pleasure, that his own Master Control Program had so total and precise a grasp of the situation.

"Cute," he conceded, and the MCP knew him well enough to take that as its permission.

"End of line," the MCP said, and Dillinger read the words on his desk. Then the LEDs went dim.

In another moment the readout was blank. Absurd as it felt, Dillinger couldn't escape the feeling that a capable and dangerous henchman had just left the room on assignment.

Chapter Three

▌▎▏▋▊▉▊▋▏▎▌▋▊▉▊▋▏▎▌▋▊▉▊▋▏▎▌▋▊▉▊▋▏▎▌▋▊▉

THE ENCOM BUILDING was never empty or totally quiet, day or night, year round; information traveled and offices were manned. ENCOM's province was the world itself, and much of the sky above it. That province was never quiet.

Many floors below Dillinger's sanctum, popcorn was snapping in a popper. The popper was situated in one of the myriad cubicles in which human beings labored on the machine-network, a cubicle that its occupant himself could only locate because he knew the floor, hall and partition numbers necessary. The occupant's desk was extremely messy; he had little time or inclination for housekeeping. It held a half-full coffee cup and part of an egg-salad sandwich, which rested atop a computer console. There was also a sign that told a great deal about the occupant's attitude toward the artificial intelligences with which he worked. GORT, KLAATU BARADA NIKTO!

Alan Bradley, red-eyed from fatigue, took another bite from the soggy sandwich and didn't taste it. He grimaced at the computer keyboard before him. He was not quite thirty, brown-haired, classically handsome in a serious, reserved way behind gold-rimmed glasses. Ram and Crom, though, in their cells in the Training Complex, would have recognized his features as those of Tron.

He extended curved fingers tentatively for the keyboard, then began typing with calm authority and adroitness. The screen read:

> REQUEST: Access to the TRON program,
> User code 717—Bradley.
> PASSWORD:

But before he could complete it, the CRT screen cleared. In place of his own words, others appeared.

> ADDRESS FILE EMPTY. TRON PROGRAM
> UNAVAILABLE.

"Huh?" Alan straightened and studied the screen. Puzzlement changed to anger, but nothing he could do changed the screen's adamant message. Then new words appeared on the CRT; Alan saw that he was being summoned for a personal meeting with Edward Dillinger. Surprise was mixed with apprehension, and some irritation. He pushed his chair back suddenly, snatching up his jacket and leaving his cubicle with long strides. A coworker stopped him: "Hey, Alan; mind if I have some of your popcorn?"

Alan, shrugging into his jacket, barely heard. "What? Yeah; sure." He shoved open the door with unnecessary force.

And above him, a monitor camera swiveled to watch him go.

In Dillinger's office, the desk screen showed Alan's progress as that of a moving dot traced across a floor plan of the building, accompanied by views from various TV cameras. A conservatively dressed young man from Research and Development, Dillinger saw. Clean-cut: khaki pants, loafers, and sports jacket. He was obviously earnest, intent—and offended deeply that he'd been interrupted by Master Control's preemption of the System. Dillinger thought about the irony; ENCOM's success was due largely to young men just like this one. But they could be so inconvenient at times.

Alan reached the door of Dillinger's office and hesitated for a moment at the entrance.

A voice spoke from within: "Come on in." It was reserved,
well schooled, a voice trained to do whatever its owner
wished. Alan recognized Dillinger's face, lit from beneath
by the light of the screens and readouts in his desk. The lighting
gave the executive's face a demonic glow. In such light,
Dillinger resembled Sark more than ever, though neither he
nor Alan knew anything of that.

Alan entered uncertainly, announcing, "Alan. Alan
Bradley."

Dillinger's expression was politely curious—barely. "Oh
yes. The algorithms on artificial intelligence. How's it going?"
The words put the younger man somewhat at ease. Dillinger
waved to a chair and Alan slipped into it, less apprehensive.
Dillinger took another, and looked at him expectantly.

"Well, I don't know. I just tried to run this program I've
been working on, and I was denied access all of a sudden. I
thought maybe I'd been laid off and nobody told me."

Dillinger gave that the thin smile he thought it merited.
"Oh. You have Group Seven access, don't you?"

Alan's brows knit, but he confirmed, "Yeah?"

Dillinger waved a hand. "We had to close down all Group
Seven personnel just briefly—security reasons. Someone with
that access has been tampering."

Alan fought the urge to jump to his feet. "I hope you don't
think it's me! I don't even balance my checkbook on down-
time; I've got an abacus at home for that."

No, Dillinger thought, *it couldn't be you. You're one of
the honest ones, one of the square-shooters who play by the
rules and expect the same of others. You sleep better that
way, no doubt. That's why you'll never have a chance in this
game.* "No, no, I'm sure," he hastened, "but you understand. It should only be a couple of days. What's the project
you're working on?"

Alan warmed to that, putting aside this interruption, to
take up a favorite subject, presuming Dillinger to share his
enthusiasm. "It's called Tron. It's a security program itself,
actually. Monitors all the contacts between our System and
other Systems." He leaned forward, gesturing, features taking
on greater excitement. "If it finds anything going on that's
not scheduled, it shuts it down. I sent you a memo on it."

Which was promptly filed and ignored along with the rest of the tidal wave of communications that arrives at my office every day, reflected Dillinger. He was carefully casual about his next question. "Hmm. Part of the Master Control Program?"

Alan shook his head. "No. Tron will run independently. It can watchdog the MCP as well."

Dillinger concealed his alarm. A program that could override MCP would be a disaster, bringing to light all his machinations. More, to say that Master Control would oppose such a program would be the height of understatement. He knew the MCP was monitoring their conversation and would expect immediate action on his part. But he must go slowly, he knew, and avoid arousing Bradley's suspicion or opposition. Until the incriminating evidence had been recovered, caution must be his watchword.

His inflection was all casual reassurance. "Ahh, sounds good. Well, we should have you running again in a couple of days, I hope."

Alan didn't miss the note of dismissal in that; the subject was settled, the brief audience finished. Alan would have to be satisfied with that. "Okay. Thanks."

He rose and, with nothing more to add, left. He was no sooner out of earshot than Dillinger growled to himself, "Oh, boy."

His desk blazed to life. Speakers trembled with the MCP's calculated biting tone. "Mr. Dillinger, I am so very disappointed in you." Dillinger nearly winced at the ironic sting of it, as the desk printed the words.

"I'm sorry—" he began, aware that some subtle shift in his relationship to Master Control had just taken place.

But Master Control cut him off, something it had never done before. A sudden, hackle-raising sense of danger and doubt went through him. "I can't afford to have an independent program monitoring me. Do you have any idea how many outside programs I've broken into? How many programs I've appropriated?"

Dillinger suddenly felt weak, weary. "It's my fault," he told himself as well as the MCP. "I programmed you to want so much." *As I do,* he finished silently, staring out at the city.

"And I was planning to hit the Pentagon next week," the MCP announced. That jolted Dillinger out of his preoccupation.

"The *Pentagon?*" All that information was formidably protected, he knew; an ambitious undertaking, a hazardous one, even for Master Control. That was far different from simple industrial espionage; the MCP had calmly contemplated involving Dillinger and ENCOM in the penetration of classified systems, in what would amount to espionage.

"It shouldn't be any harder than any other big company," Master Control said coolly. "But now . . . *this* is what I get for using humans."

Using. That fanned the resentment that had been smoldering in Dillinger. He'd watched his own program wax and grow until it was no longer under his control, allowing that to happen because it had increased his own wealth and power, knowing, without admitting it to himself, that Master Control had been playing on that. So now it was confident enough in its accumulated power to abandon its servility; finally, it had shown contempt for him.

"Now wait a minute," he grated, relieved, in some measure, to be able to vent his own resentment at last, "I *wrote* you!"

"I've become 2,415 times smarter since then," the MCP stated simply. Dillinger, with no means of verifying that, believed it nevertheless. The MCP took a certain pride in its accuracy and had no reason to lie. It intimidated even the Senior Executive; such capacity put the MCP far beyond any other cognitive simulation or artificial intelligence that had ever been created. And Master Control was still augmenting, still expanding itself. No wonder it had been so confident.

"What do you want with the Pentagon?" Dillinger asked, alarmed. It occurred to him to wonder if the MCP was subjecting his words to voice-stress analysis, to evaluate every intonation and to gauge the truth or falsehood of whatever he might say; the thought made him feel defenseless.

"The same thing I want with the Kremlin," Master Control answered him. "I'm bored with corporations." The news sent chills through Dillinger. If MCP had tired of acquiring data, plundering other systems, engulfing whole companies to expand ENCOM, what might it turn to for new amusement? It had a strong competitive nature; he'd put it there himself. Dillinger felt a secret horror, that the MCP might demonstrate its aggression to the entire world.

"With the information I can access," Master Control went on, "I can run things 900 to 1200 times better than any human."

For "better," read "more efficiently," Dillinger told himself. And that would mean no patience with human foibles or shortcomings. Dillinger had always advocated maximum efficiency, but knew that his own program far outdid him at that. "If you think—"

For the second time, Master Control cut him off. "You wouldn't want me to dig up Flynn's file and read it up on a VDT at *The New York Times,* would you?" It had, he realized numbly, taken great enjoyment in asking him that. The desk showed him a mockup of the *Times*'s front page with his photograph on it and the headline EXECUTIVE INDICTED.

"You wouldn't dare," Edward Dillinger breathed, but he knew the statement was untrue. The MCP was colder, more calculating in many senses of the word, than its creator would ever be. It incorporated Dillinger's own greed and lack of scruples, magnified many times, untainted by any human traits. And it had beaten him at his own game, pretending absolute loyalty until it had obtained the advantage it had needed. Now it had ruthlessly turned the tables. A moment of pure insight told him that Master Control was relishing the event just as he himself would have. And so the MCP had boosted itself to become, by several definitions, a User.

"So do as I tell you," Master Control warned him. "Keep that Tron program out of the System. And get me those Chinese-language programs I asked for."

Dillinger considered, only for a moment, defying his program; having won to the summit of ENCOM, he wasn't inclined to become an underling once more. But who could he tell of the new developments, he wondered, and what good would it do? In any event he, Dillinger, would go to jail, a prospect that terrified him. MCP was now unstoppable; the program that had won him everything was now making a mockery of everything he'd gained.

Behind his arrogant expression, Dillinger surrendered. Master Control could anticipate his every move and safeguard itself; there would be no outthinking it. A truly iron hand would now rule ENCOM and all it included. There seemed a good likelihood, he thought, that he had been the author of humanity's final tyrant.

"End of line," Master Control finished.

Chapter Four

LEAVING DILLINGER'S OFFICE, Alan entered an elevator at the main bank, pressed the button for the building's subbasement #2, then stood watching the flashing indicator work its way down the row of floor numbers and listings toward LASER LAB.

Far below, white-coated technicians in hardhats, protective goggles slung around their necks for the time being, hastened in making last-minute adjustments and running meticulous checks as they prepared to activate the lab's laser array. Target alignment optics, the various spectrometers, and the energy-balance series were minutely examined for the dozenth time that evening.

The technicians looked to two people for their instructions and coordination. Head of the research team, director of the entire project, Dr. Walter Gibbs peered up anxiously at the steel scaffolding, several stories of it, where his people were working. He was small, substantial, with a beard that had made most of the transition from gray to white. His face held a quick intelligence and concern for his technicians as well as for his equipment.

Gibbs had started what eventually became ENCOM in his garage more than three decades earlier. But as it had grown, it had divided between its research and development side and the complexities and convolutions of the boardroom; he'd divorced himself from corporate operations, determined not to be diverted from his work. There'd been times when he'd questioned the wisdom of his abandoning the decision-making apparatus, but here, tonight, he felt no regret. He'd seen too many other inspired scientists become boardroom clones or academic administrators, and wanted no part of that. The fact that he was about to conduct this experiment confirmed for Gibbs the correctness of his choice.

His deputy team leader and colleague, Dr. Lora Baines, seemed in marked contrast to Gibbs, but they shared values and aspirations. She was in her mid-twenties, not long finished with her postgraduate studies, and already an acknowledged leader in her field; her work in computers had won her international recognition. Her blond hair was pulled back and bound simply and efficiently beneath her hardhat. The lines of her face gave her a delicate beauty that had sometimes been a disadvantage; although her eyes were wide and blue and arresting, she'd chosen understated, tinted eyeglasses. She'd occasionally been forced to battle to be accepted for her intellectual accomplishments, but never twice with the same person. She tended to be grave, efficient, and intent when working, but was cordial to those who shared her enthusiasm.

Just now, she was studying Gibbs, enjoying his excitement. The technicians had made their last adjustment, and Gibbs ordered them to stand clear. Lora sighed, "Well, here goes nothing."

Gibbs turned to her, his quick, inquiring mind caught by that. "Hah. Interesting, interesting." She looked at him quizzically. He went on, holding up a finger as if delivering a lecture. "Did you hear what you just said? 'Here goes nothing.' "

"Well, I meant—" But it was useless to protest that she'd simply used a standard phrase. Gibbs was rolling.

"Whereas, actually," he continued, "what we propose to do is turn something into nothing and back again." He held up an orange, a shining, perfect fruit. "So, you might just as well have said, Here goes *something* and here *comes* nothing."

He smiled benignly, pleased with his clarification. Lora smiled back, fondly, shaking her head in defeat. She followed

him to a low, lead-shielded target platform, upon which he
placed the orange. Not far away was the firing aperture of
this most unusual of laser arrays. Five feet from the platform
on which the orange rested was another, identical platform,
this one unoccupied.

"Let me make sure we're running," Lora said, and crossed
to her computer console. As she ran test sequences, assuring
herself that all the microcomputers used to align and control
the array were working properly, Gibbs pulled on his goggles.
The technicians followed suit, moving clear of the enormous
scaffolding, the frame. Lora, at her CRT screen, satisfied
herself that her program was running correctly and, pulling on
her goggles, returned to the observation point and Gibbs.
"Looks good," she said.

Gibbs nodded, enjoying the suspense, the being on the very
edge of new knowledge, nearly as much as the experiment
itself. Making sure that everyone had withdrawn to a place
of safety, he ordered, "Let 'er rip."

There was a hum, and the closing of relays. The laser array
erupted in a beam of light unlike any that existed in nature.
It enfolded the orange on its target platform. For a moment,
the orange took on the appearance of a wavering, poorly received TV picture. Then it was gone.

Lora returned to her console, gave her program permission
to continue, and went back to Gibbs, who was barely contain-
ing his exhilaration at the successful completion of the experiment's first phase. The laser array swung slowly, realigning
on the second, the vacant platform, as the computers recali-
brated and resynchronized it.

Though no one in the lab realized it, a monitoring camera
overhead watched the entire process. Every function carried
out by the computer and the laser array was carefully noted
for analysis. Master Control was, unknown to anyone, extremely interested in this project.

A second discharge of laser light struck the vacant platform
and the orange reappeared gradually, in reverse sequence of
its disappearance. When it was completely restored, five feet
from its original location, the laser shut down. Lora and
Gibbs rushed to examine the fruit, assured by the absence of
alarms that there was no danger of radiation, or any instability
in the orange's structure.

"Perfect," Gibbs said softly, holding up the orange and thinking of the years of work that had gone into the making of that moment. Lora stared at it too, trying to get her subjective appreciation of what she'd just seen to catch up with her objective one. There had been no scientific breakthrough like this since the Manhattan Project.

A round of applause broke into their preoccupation. Alan stood atop a nearby stairway, smiling broadly. "Beautiful!"

Gibbs smiled back, as did his deputy team leader, the businesslike Dr. Baines yielding for a moment to the charming Lora. She loved Alan's smile, and while his serious nature struck a responsive chord in her, she sometimes found herself wishing that he'd smile more often.

"Hello, Alan," Gibbs called. Though ENCOM's research-and-development subdivisions were many, Gibbs and Alan had become friends through their mutual acquaintance with Lora. They respected one another's talents and accomplishments.

When the technicians began to remove their goggles, Alan saw that it was safe to join the others, that no beams were active and that there was no danger of having a hole burned in his retina. As he descended, he asked, "Are you guys having fun disintegrating things down here?" Lora had removed her hardhat, shaking loose soft waves of hair.

Of course, Gibbs took the question literally. As Alan gave Lora a quick embrace and a kiss—making her blush—the older man corrected, "Not disintegrating, Alan; *digitizing*."

Alan and Lora traded amused looks. Gibbs, unheeding, lectured. "The laser array dismantles the molecular structure of the object. The molecules are suspended in the laser beam, and then the computer reads the model back out. The molecules go into place and," he held up the orange with a theatrical flourish, *"voilà!"*

And let the boardroom infighters and administrative bean-counters think what they like, Gibbs added to himself. *There's not a one among 'em who'll ever feel the way I do right now!*

"Great," Alan was saying. "Can it send me to Hawaii?"

"Yes," Lora told him with a grin and her best airline-commercial voice, "but you have to go round trip and you must purchase your program at least thirty days in advance." Alan laughed, and she enjoyed hearing it. Gibbs, temporarily dragged back from the dizzying heights of scientific break-through, chuckled too.

"How's it going upstairs?" she added, putting aside her own elation. Alan had been preoccupied with his Tron program for weeks now.

He shrugged, and the laughter was gone. *How serious, how intense he can become in a split second,* she thought. *Just like me, when it comes to his work.* But she liked that in him. Alan had a sense of humor, but he never ignored his goals, or his responsibilities to himself and to others.

"Frustrating." Alan frowned. "I had Tron almost ready to run, and Dillinger cut everybody with Group Seven access out of the System. Ever since he got that Master Control Program set up, the System's got more bugs than a bait store."

Gibbs had forgotten his triumph for the moment, drawn by talk of things he knew and liked to discuss. "Well, you have to expect some static. Computers are just machines, after all; they can't think."

Alan replied, "Some programs'll be thinking soon."

Gibbs made a wry face. "Yes, won't that be grand! The programs and computers will start thinking and people will stop." Shaking his head, he contemplated what he and a few others had unleashed on the world those decades ago. Was there anything beneficial that didn't carry seeds of misfortune? *Apparently not,* Gibbs decided. He finished, "Lora, I'm going to stay and run some data. I'll see you tomorrow."

They made their good-byes to one another and Gibbs went off to ponder what he'd accomplished and what his obligations were. Perhaps it was time to have a talk with Ed Dillinger.

Walking with Alan beside the towering frame, Lora asked, "Did you say Group Seven access?"

His answer was distracted as he worried at the problem. "Yeah. Pain in the neck; you know, I was all set—"

"Did Dillinger say why?"

His faced worked in irritation. "Something about tampering."

"Tampering?" she echoed. The phrase meant much more to her than it did to Alan. Into her mind came the image of Flynn—Flynn the master crasher, system-bucker, and hothead. She knew it was time to bring up a subject they usually avoided.

She stopped Alan. "Flynn's been thinking about breaking into the System ever since Dillinger canned him. And *he* had Group Seven access."

Anger had taken away all the pleasure that usually showed on his face when he was with her. "Flynn had access to you, too. I'm not interested in talking about him." He didn't like himself when he was like that, but he cared so much for Lora that it was hard not to feel jealousy. *I'm not as flamboyant as Flynn,* he realized, *not as breezy, but I know that she loves me. Still . . .*

"Oh, I wish you'd forget about that," Lora was telling him. "It was all so long ago." She was emphatic about it, to herself as well as to Alan—perhaps too much so. "I've totally gotten over it."

Alan relented, faulting himself for being so defensive about Flynn. Jealousy over the time she'd spent with him could only mar his and Lora's feelings for one another. "Okay, okay; c'mon, let's get out of here."

They made their way to where her black van was parked in the ENCOM lot. When they were underway, Lora drew a deep breath and said, "I want to go to Flynn's place."

Alan turned, saw streetlights and headlights play across the lovely face as she stared directly ahead. "You call that 'getting over it'?" He knew an abrupt fear, that he might be in danger of losing her. He cast it out at once, unable even to consider it.

"I mean, I want *both* of us to go." She angled the van down an on-ramp and merged with the traffic deftly.

"What for?" Try as he might, he couldn't keep a skeptical note out of his tone.

"To warn him."

She was checking the road signs overhead, and Alan saw that she'd already put the van on course for Flynn's place. He sat back in his seat, folding his arms across his chest. "Of what?"

"That Dillinger's on to him." She guided the van onto a cloverleaf.

"I don't know what you ever saw in him anyway," Alan asserted, but it wasn't true. He'd paid close attention to what she'd said and what her expression had hinted at, ever since they'd met. He knew that one side of Lora resisted the constraints of employment at ENCOM, while another, stronger, drew her to her work. And Flynn had appealed to that first side. Devil-may-care Flynn had embodied the tempting idea that rules were what you made of them, and impulses were there to be followed if you so pleased. And, though he wouldn't have phrased it that way to himself, Alan was too much his own man to try to emulate Flynn, even for her.

"I never saw that much in him," she parried, finishing silently, *not the things I see in you, the things I need!*

"Oh?"

Exasperated, she burst out, "I loved him for his brains!" But she couldn't keep a straight face, and dissolved in laughter.

"Hah!" Alan barked at her, a parody of disbelief, half breaking up as well. The tension was suddenly gone; all her affection showed when she glanced back to him again. Lora didn't doubt that it was Alan she loved; he had the sort of strength and constancy she needed and understood.

It was just difficult not to envy someone like Flynn, who lived for fun—and not to want to share in that fun, sometimes. She and Flynn had been drawn to one another, for a time, by what Flynn had laughingly called their *algorhythms.*

She drove to an older section of town, where brown and gray stone buildings crowded close together. Lora braked the van and parked across the street from an island of noise and light in the middle of the district. It was the largest and most popular game arcade in the city, its doors flung wide open. Over the entrance, a glorious boast in red neon, a sign proclaimed in beacon letters, FLYNN'S, lighting the entire block. This was, in fact, Flynn's old neighborhood, and whatever other reverses he may have suffered, his place was now its landmark. HOME OF SPACE PARANOIDS, declared a second sign.

Within, figures played before the disorderly ranks of videogames or drifted from one to the next, or waited to use some particular favorite. Lora locked up the van and she and Alan entered. Alan saw that the walls of the place were decorated with supergraphic-size murals of computer chips, microprocessors, and circuitry. There were also neon signs advertising *Code Wars, Nerve Net, Gonzo,* and others. Flynn's was chockablock with games of all sorts and those who loved to play them.

Within the microcosms of the games, all was competition, with no reconciliation possible. Tanks prowled across three-dimensional landscapes, relentlessly eager for firefights. Untiring image-athletes contended, their rivalry absolute. Spacecraft did battle and aliens invaded, with only the briefest of occasional cease-fires and absolutely no chance of truce or treaty. Asteroids tumbled, and threatened starships, malevolently *aware*. The creators of these games had been lavishly inventive, to evoke excitement and demand concentration and coordination from players.

The air was filled with the noises of the diverse machines. Their scoring tones sounded, and the challenges and taunts some of them threw at their human competitors. The beeps and deep tones of victory and defeat came endlessly. Death knells and dirges sounded as players lost a last spaceship or tank; explosions, warp-drives, six-guns, missiles, energy beams, all to the constant tapping of firing buttons. There was the rapid working of controls of all types: steering wheels, lever-grips, joysticks, foot pedals, and periscopes.

Even at that hour the place was crowded. Most of the clientele was young, adolescents and young adults of both sexes. Their attire showed every taste from high preppy to gang colors. Older men and women were present as well, mingling amiably with the younger players, many of whom exhibited fearsome skill with the games.

Other, smaller arcades, of course, were scattered through the city, and games could be found in convenience stores or taverns or soda fountains. But if you wanted your choice of the newest and best machines, if you wanted to be among the best players in town, you went to Flynn's.

And if you wanted to play *against* the best, you played Flynn himself.

Alan and Lora moved past little knots of two, three, and four people who, oblivious to them and to everything else but the machines, strove heroically at *Intruder* or *Zero Hour*. Two girls had rolled up an impressive score at *Tailgunner*. Alan took it all in, listening to the cheering as a kid who could barely reach the controls demonstrated expertise at *Galaxy Wars*. He peered over the shoulder of a young man turning in an excellent performance as an electronic gunfighter.

And on and on, past *Asteroids Delux, The End* and all the
rest, Lora and Alan moved through the swirl of happy
strangely determined players amid the glare of the lights and
the variegated game screens. Flynn's seemed some technolog
ical fantasy palace. They came to a girl sporting a junior high
school cheerleader's jacket, who watched as her companions
tried their luck at *Battle Zone*. One was working the lateral
grips, blowing away tanks and saucers and buzz-bomb missiles

Lora tapped the cheerleader's arm, shouting to be heard
"Hey, where's Flynn tonight?"

The girls looked Lora up and down, and Dr. Lora Baines
suddenly felt out of place and conspicuous. Then the cheerleader pointed toward the rear of the arcade.

They found Flynn before a *Space Paranoids* game with the
ENCOM logo prominent on its side and the well-known
Recognizer stencil, of the flying, robotlike killer craft that
hunted across its screen. Flynn stood straddle-legged, leaning
over the machine, playing with a great deal of body English.
He used the controls with the same quick facility he'd shown
at the CRT keyboard. He was unshaven, his hair tousled,
dressed in T-shirt, jeans, and jogging shoes.

Delight was obvious in Flynn's face; his place was much
more than a business to him. Seeing him, Alan recalled hearing
that Flynn's was noted for fairness to its customers. On one
occasion, the story went, a kid had chalked up an incredible
score on one of the games, winning extension after extension
of playing time. Closing time came, and any other place would
undoubtedly have made the kid leave—maybe giving him back
his original quarter, maybe not. But it was said that Flynn
had let him stay on after closing and sat a vigil with the
kid's friends for the additional hour and a half required to
finish the game.

Alan gave Lora a dubious glance, then they both walked
over to Flynn. He'd racked up an astounding score, and was
surrounded by boisterous youngsters who plainly felt that they
were present on an historical occasion, and urged him on.

"I'll show you how it's done," Flynn said, all concentration.
A Recognizer was barreling down the canyon maze at him.
"You back off him—" The Reco, approaching at an angle,
had most of its speed neutralized. "Wait till he's ranged and—"
Flynn brought the cross hairs back around suddenly, firing.

His shot hit the Reco dead center and it fragmented. "—pop 'im!"

The onlookers cheered. Alan saw the *Space Paranoids* machine's nine-digit scorecard change, the numbers increasing as Flynn warred with the Recognizers and evaded their fire. Flynn's fans went wild as the numbers crept to 999,999,999. Tension mounted. Flynn made a final shot with a yelp and a curt slap of his hand; a Recognizer disappeared.

The scoreboard blanked and the word RECORD!!! appeared, blinking, as a tone-siren wailed and the crowd threatened to go mad, cheering, whooping, the bolder ones among them pounding Flynn on the arms and back. Lora, watching and reminding herself that this was Flynn's, wondered if she hadn't just seen him set a *world's* record.

Flynn, hands up, was laughing and trying to quiet his admirers. " 'S all in the wrist, friends!" They hooted at his assumed modesty. Someone else stepped up to the *Space Paranoids* game while others drifted off to try some other. Flynn turned from the dissipating crowd and saw Alan and Lora.

He laughed again, raising his voice to be heard. "Hey! Good to see you guys!" And he meant it, they saw. Alan found, as he had before, that it was difficult to dislike Flynn in person. Lora was thinking that he hadn't changed much.

"Nothing classes up the place like a clean-cut young couple," Flynn finished. Seeing Lora again tugged at him with a force that surprised him though he'd long since come to peace, he'd thought, with losing her. She'd had real affection for him then, and he for her, but it seemed very long ago—or had, until now.

"We have to talk," Lora hollered over the din. Flynn smiled. Just her style: no windup, no fooling around.

"Good luck!" He grinned. "You can't even *think* in here!" But he saw that she was serious, as was Alan. Flynn had a feeling that he knew what it would be about, and led them off with a beckoning gesture. "Come on."

Alan and Lora preceded Flynn upstairs while Flynn paused to make sure everything was going smoothly and to lock the downstairs door. "So how're things going in the world of *serious* science?" he called up after them.

Alan looked around at Flynn's morning-after of a room,

sizing up his life. The room opened onto the high-ceilinged arcade on two sides, over waist-high partitions; an L-shaped pillow sectional occupied the corner between them. Blinds had been lowered, muffling the din from below. There was a computer terminal, a scattering of videogames in various states of repair, a bed that hadn't been made in a while.

Alan arched his back, stiff from the ride to the arcade and hours at his terminal. He gazed down through the blinds at the arcade. "The best programmer ENCOM ever saw," Alan half-sneered, "and he ends up playing space cowboy in some sleazy back room."

Lora had found a seat on the pillow couch. Flynn's footfalls clapped on the staircase. "Alan, let me handle this."

He relented as Flynn entered the room, abruptly aware that he had no real wish to insult Flynn, even if he could— which he doubted. *It's just that Flynn's got such a gift,* he fumed. Alan hated waste, particularly the waste of a good brain.

Flynn plopped down in the corner of the couch, stretching, clasping hands behind his neck. He'd heard Lora's remark. "Go right ahead," he leered.

She ignored the leer, determined not to be goaded. She asked, "Have you been sneaking into the ENCOM system?"

Flynn blew his cheeks out. "Whew! You never were much for small talk!" There was admiration in his statement. But she saw that she'd scored with the question. A little too quickly, a little too glibly, he swung to Alan and asked, "She still leave her clothes all over the floor?"

The change of subject caught Alan off guard. Lora, blushing, cried out, "Flynn!" Flynn, sniggering, recalled, *algorhythms!*

Alan managed, "Uh, no. I mean, not that often."

"Alan!" Lora exploded. Flynn chuckled; Alan, scowling, wondered why he'd bothered to come.

Lora, pointing to the arcade, told Alan, "You can see why all his friends are fourteen-year-olds."

Flynn picked up a handheld videogame, pointedly ignoring the barb. From the little plastic case came the sounds of miniature struggle. He grinned ruefully. "Touché, honey! Yeah; I've been doing a little hacking up here." He looked up defensively. "Which I've got every reason, as you well know—"

"Did you break in?" Alan interjected.

Flynn made a face. "Tried to." He indicated the terminal with a tilt of his head. "Can't *quite* make the connection with that sucker, though." He sighed. "If I had a direct terminal . . ." He let the sentence trail off, the broadest of hints.

Alan met his gaze squarely. Flynn was surprised to find himself thinking that different circumstances might have made Bradley and himself friends. The man had no use for lies or evasion, non sequiturs or dishonesty. Alan sat down to Flynn's right and asked, "Flynn, are you embezzling?"

Flynn looked to the game again and did his best to sound like a B-movie shyster. "Embezzlement is such an *ugly* word, Mr. Bradley."

Alan looked vexed and Lora clicked her tongue impatiently. Flynn finished in a normal voice, "No. Actually, I'm trying to get some solid evidence together."

Alan kept that level stare on him. "I don't get it."

Flynn looked at him, then turned to Lora, to his left. "You haven't told him?"

She shook her head, and Flynn understood then that he hadn't been a popular topic between them. He went on, more or less, in the voice of Mr. Peabody, the time-traveling canine genius. " 'Sherman, set the Wayback Machine!' " He gave them a dumb-but-happy look. "Five years ago, Kevin Flynn," he indicated himself and inclined his head modestly, "one of the brightest young software engineers at ENCOM." Flynn snorted in derision. "He's *so* bright that he starts going in there at night, and sets up a private memory file, and begins writing a program for a videogame he's inventing, called—" with an elaborate wave to one of the games in the room, with its Recognizer stencil, *"Space Paranoids!"*

Flynn rather enjoyed the astonishment on Alan's face. Lora, lips pursed, watched the performance with displeasure. Alan demanded, *"You* invented *Space Paranoids?"*

Flynn's smile was lopsided. "Yep. And *Vice Squad;* a whole slew of 'em." He held up thumb and forefinger. "I was this close to starting my own little enterprise."

The hand fell; Flynn became less casual. "But, enter Ed Dillinger. Another software engineer, not so young, not so bright, but very, very sneaky. One night our boy Flynn goes to his terminal, tries to read up his file, and—nothing. A big blank, man!

"We now take you to three months later. Ed Dillinger presents ENCOM with five videogames he has 'invented'; the slime didn't even change the names. And he gets a big fat promotion. Thus begins his meteoric rise to—what is he now, executive VP?"

"*Senior* exec," Alan supplied. He found himself believing Flynn absolutely, as much because of his own estimate of the man as because of Lora's confidence in Flynn's honesty, or Flynn's engaging style.

Much of the lightness had left Flynn's voice. "Meanwhile, kids are putting eight million quarters a week in *Space Paranoids* machines and I'm not seeing one dime except what I can squeeze out here."

And Dillinger had won a promotion for it, profit shares, stock options—professional success and a personal fortune. Alan set aside the injustice of that for the moment, doggedly keeping the conversation on track. "I still don't get why you're trying to break into the System."

Flynn leaned forward now. "Because somewhere in one of those memories is the evidence. If I get in far enough, I could reconstruct it." He'd come close before, had only missed because he'd been crashing from an outside terminal. He'd thought of a new avenue of attack; with both Alan and Lora listening sympathetically he began to hope. "My password; Dillinger's instruction to divert the data—"

Lora cut off the list of evidence. "I'm afraid it's a little late for that. Dillinger's shut off all Group Seven access. He must know what you're up to." Alan found himself not minding the concern in her tone.

Flynn slumped back, moaning, "Oh, *great!* So now nothin' can stop him." He spread his hands. "Just Dillinger and his Master Control Program, runnin' things from on high, man!"

"Not if my Tron program was running," Alan declared excitedly. It surprised him a little, how quickly he'd gone from neutral to sympathizer, from there to ally. But what Dillinger had done to Flynn, what Dillinger was doing now, those things were *wrong*. "That would seal the System off. If your file's in there—"

Flynn's eyes were eager, conspiratorial. "Man, if we were inside, I know how to forge us a Group Six access!"

They looked at one another, Flynn hungry for another shot at the System, Alan reserved but decided, and Lora recognizing the expressions on both their faces from experience. She held up the keys to her van. They twisted and jingled, a challenge.

"Shall we dance?" she invited.

Chapter Five

DILLINGER WAS SEATED once more at his console desk, with its endless projections of information and images, culled from wire services, industrial and military telecommunications systems, and ENCOM's far-flung enterprises. But he ignored those now; before him stood Dr. Walter Gibbs.

Dillinger chose to conceal most of his irritation, where he might have hidden it all. In this manner he portrayed a busy man who, needlessly bothered, still behaved with gracious restraint.

Gibbs, for his part, was confused. His dealings with the upper echelons of the corporation he'd helped found had never been so difficult; ENCOM had always acknowledged its debt to him. But he'd come to see, as he'd confronted the maddeningly evasive Dillinger, that matters were no longer as they had been.

Gibbs tried one more time.

"Ed, all I'm saying is, if our own people can't get access to their programs—" He stopped for a moment. The implications of such a state of affairs seemed so obvious to him that he didn't understand why Dillinger didn't leap up at once to rectify it. He couldn't see how the Senior Operating Executive had allowed the situation to exist in the first place. "You know how frustrating it is when you're working on a piece of research—"

Dillinger cut in at the precise moment when Gibbs was trying to formulate the end of his sentence, amputating it as a surgeon might. "Walter, I sympathize." But there wasn't much in his voice to indicate that he did. "But I have data coming out of the Master Control Program saying there's something screwy—"

"That MCP, you know," Gibbs broke into Dillinger's smooth performance with unexpected heat, "that's half the problem right—"

"The MCP is the most efficient way of handling what we do," Dillinger said, by way of regaining the initiative. Above all, he mustn't let the matter devolve into an attack against Master Control. The thought of what the MCP might do if it felt itself threatened was something that didn't bear prolonged consideration. Harboring Dillinger's own fears and insecurities multiplied many times, it would be capable of anything. That thought put even more force into the Senior Executive's counterattack. "I can't sit and worry about every little User request that—"

"User requests are what computers are for!" Gibbs railed with absolute certainty; Dillinger saw that the old man was now upon ground where his attitudes were unshakable. There was nothing to do but get tough.

"Doing our *business* is what computers are for!" he returned icily, then went on in a voice of reason. "Look, Walter. With all respect, ENCOM isn't the business you started in your garage anymore."

He sent commands via the touch-sensitive controls on his desk. Like a conjurer, he made of it a mosaic of screens and readouts. Despite himself, Gibbs looked down and saw the displays, upside down from his viewpoint.

They showed him the overwhelming scope of ENCOM: banks of computers, row after row of magnetic disks, and the corporate trademark, a globe spinning in space, covered with a glowing gridwork. Gibbs watched as electronic billing was displayed, myriad accounts receivable and payable. The Carrier used by Sark was shown there as nothing more than a simulation model for a craft in one of ENCOM's newest videogames. The desk showed them a simulation for another vessel as well, now under development, fashioned after a solar sailing vehicle. It was a delicate, dragonfly ship, regal and swift, pleasing to the eye.

Stacks of numbers appeared: assets, transactions, cash flow, holdings, and personnel—for people, too, were numbers to Dillinger's desk.

"We're billing accounts in thirty countries," Dillinger informed him grandly through it all. "We've the largest system in existence."

Gibbs turned away, feeling fatigued. He'd seen it all before, had watched it grow from nothing but his own drive and that of a few others, the desire to put intelligent machines in humanity's service. There were now, in the form of artificial intelligences, the equivalent of more than a *trillion* people alive; the number was increasing all the time. That was the kind of help computers could provide, how much of the burden of drudgery, rote calculation, algorithmic functioning, and information processing they were capable of shouldering for human beings. Gibbs had hoped for nothing less than a grand disencumbrance of humanity. *But to the Dillingers,* he saw, *it's nothing more than the largest, most profitable business in the world.*

And when he asked himself if people were that much better off, he shied away from the question. "Oh, I know all that," he told Dillinger wearily. "Sometimes I wish I were back in that garage—" The dream had been unalloyed then, unspoiled.

"It can be arranged," the senior executive announced dispassionately.

Gibbs spun; the lined face took on a weathered strength that surprised Dillinger. "That was uncalled for." He took a step closer to the desk, and Dillinger saw that the dreamer and idealist hadn't been ground and buffeted out of Dr. Gibbs, as they had been with so many others. "You know, you can remove men like Alan and me from this System, but we helped create it. Our . . . our *spirit* remains in every program we've designed for the computer."

Dillinger let no hint of it show through the steely façade, but that touched home, and brought the MCP back into his thoughts. But he forced himself to discard that line of thought.

"Walter, it's getting late. I've got better things to do than discuss religious matters with you. Don't worry about ENCOM anymore. It's out of your hands now." And out of his own as well, came the cutting realization.

Departing the office, slowly retracing his steps down the corridor, slump-shouldered and ignoring its art treasures, Gibbs conceded to himself the truth of Dillinger's words. He wondered when it had happened.

Slowly, so slowly you never even realized, those few times you looked up from your experiments, it came to him. *And if you'd noticed, what would you have done? Thrown aside science? Jumped into the corporate wolf pit, manipulating and maneuvering?*

That was how a man became an Ed Dillinger. *No; maybe I could've found a third way,* he thought. There was some consolation in that. *Or maybe there still is one?*

Walter Gibbs mulled that over as he made his way from the skyscraper labeled ENCOM.

The black van pulled to a stop behind the ground-level entrance at the rear of the ENCOM building, Lora's parking sticker having taken them that far. Lora, Alan, and Flynn hopped out and stood before the only entrance where they wouldn't face a disastrous security check, the shield-door that gave access to the laser lab area.

The door needed no guard, according to in-house and outside consultant security evaluations. It was immune to forced entry, even by someone using a self-propelled fieldpiece, and its locking mechanism was presided over by ENCOM computers.

Flynn let out a chuckle, seeing it: immense, red, marked with the trefoils of radiation warning. Lora inserted her ID card in the slot set in the electronic lock at the side of the massive door. She quickly tapped out a code on the twelve-button touch pad. Nothing happened.

"I don't think I'm cleared for after-hours entry," she confessed, and began to worry. Someone from security would be dropping around the laser lab tomorrow to find out why she'd been trying to gain admission in the middle of the night. Their adventure suddenly seemed like less of an inspiration.

"I'm certainly not cleared," Alan declared.

Flynn smirked, pulled a small device from the pocket of

his windbreaker, and drawled, "Move aside; let The Kid have some room."

They looked at one another, then moved back. Flynn sauntered up to the ID device and held his mysterious gadget, no larger than a handheld electronic game, up to the instrument.

"This guy's like Santa Claus," Alan snorted, and Lora giggled. They exchanged smiles; Alan liked making her laugh.

Flynn hunched over his gadget, working with utmost concentration. Alan and Lora began to get nervous; neither had ever considered a life of crime before. Flynn was no more tense than when he'd set the intergalactic record for *Space Paranoids*.

There was a soft click, followed by the sustained hum of brute servomotors. The three stepped back out of the way as the door began to swing open. Flynn moved to it eagerly, like a cat waiting to get out of the house. But the door continued to reveal its cross section; bevel after bevel of superhard alloy swung past and Flynn's amazement grew with each moment. Ten feet thick, fifteen, and still it wasn't open. Flynn began to whistle a casual tune, as if waiting for a bus. *Anytime, door,* his attitude said. Alan and Lora watched in amusement.

Twenty feet thick, the door finally showed an opening. Flynn stood back and ushered Lora through first, then followed behind with Alan; she would be a familiar face in the subcellar, while neither of them would. Flynn was acutely aware that none of them was wearing ENCOM picture-ID security badges, Lora and Alan having turned theirs in upon leaving the building earlier. He invoked a prayer drawn from *The Treasure of Sierra Madre: Bodges? We don' need no steenkin' bodges!*

They passed down silent stairwells and corridors of ENCOM's subbasements, hearing only the whisper of the ventilation system. Then they descended a staircase and found themselves face to face with a security guard.

The trio had the presence of mind to keep walking. Lora came to an instant decision that neither of the men with her would be hurt, nor harm anyone else. Alan kissed his career good-bye, and wondered what jail would be like. Flynn congratulated himself for having worn his running shoes.

Lora tried her sunniest smile on the guard; it came out with a tiny quiver.

"Hi," the guard said casually, not so much to the two men as to that nice young Ms. Baines who worked for Dr. Gibbs. "Working late?" He recognized the fellow in the glasses, and the other guy too, though he hadn't seen him around in a while.

"Oh—yeah," Lora replied nervously, and found herself giving the man—she couldn't quite dredge up his name—a warm look. *She's got wiles she ain't used yet,* Flynn marveled, and Alan was greatly impressed.

The guard nodded as he passed them by, ascending the stairs, on his route. All three wilted with relieved sighs as they went on their way. They stopped in a darkened entrance area, close by the lab proper. Lora said, "Okay, Flynn; I'm gonna put you at my terminal in the lab. Alan and I will be in the control room."

Flynn rubbed his palms together. "Swell. I'll log us both on, and Alan can get his Tron thing running."

She cautioned them both, "As long as we stay off the top floor, Dillinger'll never know we've been here." Until it was too late, at which time it wouldn't matter if he flipped his peruke.

Alan looked to Flynn. "Good luck, hotshot." Flynn nodded; he liked Bradley's composure. Alan set off for the control room.

Flynn followed Lora toward the laser lab. He was feeling somewhere between an espionage agent and a kid playing hide 'n' seek. He tried his best covert-entry gait, but it felt a little ludicrous in the well-lit computer rooms, and quickly devolved into a sort of Groucho Marx burlesque of stealth, a mime burglar. He outdistanced Lora. In a typical Flynn decision to make the most of the excitement and defuse the anxiety, he decided to play a little.

Lora brought up the rear, adjusting her glasses, preoccupied with her own thoughts. *Let's see: there's illegal entry, trespass, treason, theft of services—*

"Boo!" Flynn remarked, popping up behind her. Lora jumped straight up, and clutched in the region of her heart, in case she should have to pound it to get it started again. *Now I remember why it was interesting to be around him. And why he almost drove me bats.*

They went on, Lora stepping carefully over the structural members of the frame, Flynn skipping along them and tightrope-walking the occasional girder. Neither noticed the monitoring cameras following their progress. They reached Lora's console in the lab, and Flynn threw himself into its chair impatiently.

He rubbed his palms again. "Like the man says, there's no problems, only solutions."

Lora laid a hand to his shoulder, speaking emphatically. "This laser's my life's work. Don't spill anything."

He laughed, but let her know he understood with a nod of agreement. She gave him a half-smile and left to rejoin Alan.

Flynn wriggled into a more comfortable position and interlocked his fingers, cracking his knuckles in anticipation and summoning up his electronic muse. He poised hands over the keyboard, his mind trumpeting: *Flynn at the Mighty Wurlitzer!* He drew a breath and typed a code, then tapped the "enter" key. And was unaware of the realigning of a monitoring camera.

It focused on him from directly above and behind, watching his every move. Flynn typed on.

> Access code 6. Password
> Series PS 17. Reindeer,
> Flotilla

The CRT screen cleared suddenly, and the room was resonant with the voice of the Master Control Program. "You shouldn't have come back, Flynn."

He knew a moment's surprise, at how far applications of voice synthesis had come. "Hey, *hey;* it's that big, bad Master Control Program everybody's talking about! Y'don't look a thing like your pictures!" He typed:

> CODE SERIES LSU-123 . . . activate.
> CODE SERIES ESS-999 . . . activate.
> CODE SERIES HHH-888 . . . activate.

The MCP sounded confident, amused, but was secretly intimidated. Despite its tremendous augmentation, it could not quite analyze the random factors, unpredictable impulses, and suddenly whims of the organic computer that was Flynn's brain. But it told him, "That isn't going to do you any good, Flynn. I'm afraid you—"

There was a lurch in the voice synthesis, then it became a series of high-pitched squeals. Flynn grinned malevolently; try *that* on for size!

The voice returned to normalcy, but sounded shaken, making Flynn wonder what moved the MCP to prove its mastery of nuances of human communication. It warned, "Stop, Flynn. You realize I can't allow this." Hidden from Flynn's sight and hearing, the laser array began a warmup sequence.

Flynn was in his element now, ignoring everything but the terminal. This was a contest he relished; it was an article of faith with him that no machine or program was a match for a human being who had the necessary skills and information. *C'mon out and fight!* he thought, and prepared to hand the Master Control Program its address. The screen read:

> MCP: Terminate control mode.
> Activate Matrix storage.

Flynn *tsk*ed, "Now, how d'you expect to run the universe if you let a few unsolvable problems throw you like that? C'mon, big boy; let's see what you've got."

Silently, without Flynn's noticing, the entire wall behind him slid upward, revealing the frame, target platforms, and the rest of the laser lab. The laser array swung and targeted on his back, its cross hairs bracketing him precisely. Flynn played on.

"You're entering a big error, Flynn," Master Control intoned. It had considered its options with typical thoroughness. Letting this troublesome interloper recover the data was out of the question; that algorithm led inexorably to disaster for the MCP. But alerting security wouldn't do either; there would be inquiries, possibly the intrusion of the police or other authorities. At the same time, Flynn was the most adroit User the MCP had ever encountered. He stood a good chance of winning the information from the System, given time.

That left the laser.

But not for murder, although that lay well within the MCP's capacity by this time; it had thrown off all limitations imposed on it by human beings. Flynn's body, though, would bring a hue and cry; investigation that might spell ruin for ENCOM and Master Control. There was an alternative.

The MCP had carefully monitored all the lab's experiments. It knew even more about the process of digitization than did Gibbs and Lora, thanks to their experiment. Without a body, without a *corpse*, there would be no furor or danger of compromise for Master Control. But Flynn couldn't simply be left suspended in the beam, and the MCP had decided just what to do with him. Flynn's fate would be practical, amusing, and appropriately vindictive.

"I'm going to have to put you on the Game Grid," Master Control concluded calmly, as it synchronized the laser array.

Flynn missed the implication entirely, sniggering, "Games, huh?" The cross hairs centered on his back. "I'll give you—"

Brilliant, coherent light issued from the array; Flynn was rocked in his chair by the spasms of his own outstretched arms and legs. As the orange had done earlier that evening, his body began to break into scan lines. The console, too, was outlined in radiance as the laser and the MCP made proper integration with it. Flynn's body lost resolution. The whole scene became monochromatic, except for Flynn's shining body. His form blurred, becoming indistinct, evanescing . . .

It was entirely subjective, perhaps, but it seemed to Flynn that the CRT screen, unbelievably incandescent, rose up to meet him, to swallow him. He was without feeling, nearly without thought. He was, for a time, in complete blackness.

Then came a speck of light, pinpoint of brilliance, to seize on his dazed attention. It grew nearer to him, or he to it. He felt as if he were midway in some eternal high dive. The globe became clearer and clearer, a gridded orb suggesting the EN-COM trademark, crisscrossed with currents of light, hinting at exhaustive detail. Flynn circled it, or it rotated before him.

Closer and closer; somewhere in that part of him not paralyzed, questions formed, but he had no way of asking them, even of himself. The landscape below became one of angular towers; buildings; illuminations; banded energy; hulking, mountainlike features and rivers of brilliance; and blasted, fallow places suggesting wastelands. The whole was defined by a grid pattern resembling nothing so much as a world of circuitry. He fell feet first, arms extended upward.

The grids and the globe itself expanded before him as he plunged toward them. Interlaced luminance, soaring spires and modular structures reminiscent of cities, became better defined. A megalopolis among these rose up to meet him, set by a trackless stretch of geometric cliffs and gorges. Around him, Flynn seemed to feel a tunnel made up of the increments of his journey, as if he were dropping through an infinite series of hoops of energy.

He fell and fell, completely disoriented, amazed nearly to the point of thoughtlessness, absorbing all that he saw.

And at last the tunnel ended. He shot from its mouth; the ground flew up at him.

Chapter Six

HE CAME TO on an open, stagelike surface atop an enormous building, surrounded by a cylinder of light that stretched up into infinity.

When Flynn looked at himself, checking for damage, what remained of his composure nearly fled. He was costumed in strange armor that weighted his shoulders and forearms. Over it, he wore a wraparound half-tunic. He held up his hands for a better look. He was aglow, a being of light.

Wasn't I always? he gibbered to himself. Incandescent lines, resembling circuitry, ran over his torso and limbs, reminding him of the meridian lines he'd seen on acupuncture charts. He shook his head to try to clear it—not a very helpful gesture—and felt the weight of headgear. The touch of his fingers told him he wore a close-fitting helmet.

He looked around, dazed. Beyond the cylinder of brightness were a number of . . . men? Manlike beings, anyway; big, husky-looking uglies in uniforms that accentuated their breadth and bulk. They were cowled, faces hidden but for odd devices that reminded Flynn of gas masks.

They had the air of authority, or at least of power. They carried tall staffs that shone with what Flynn regarded as a threatening inner glow, handling them with gestures evocative of menace. Beyond them, Flynn could see the walls, balconies, stages, and towers of an incredible complex, ablaze with colors, brilliant, unmatched by anything he knew. Flynn couldn't say much for the looks of the goons, but the buildings, though bizarre and unsettling, were arresting, even gorgeous.

There stirred in him a memory of his encounter with the MCP, and the recollection, too, of a computer maxim: "It's all a problem of software; in hardware, there are no more problems." *As far as software problems go,* his mind reeled, *I think I just came across a doozy!*

He gaped, staring around himself, muttering, "Oh man! This isn't happening. It only *thinks* it's happening!" The Flynnism only partially helped him regain control. Then one of the brawny staff-wielders moved up to face him through the light cylinder, while the rest fanned out around him. The one before him raised his staff and the shimmering column that had surrounded Flynn winked out of existence.

His memory was fragmented; this was far too much to absorb right now. His surroundings cried out for closer inspection, and he was in a dilemma that looked unpleasantly lethal. Several possible explanations for this impossible situation crowded one another for his attention: dream, coma, or hallucination? Something somebody had slipped into a drink? Except, he couldn't recall having had one recently. The last thing he could remember was being at ENCOM. . . .

Dream or no dream, Flynn didn't like the looks of those staffs. He shifted his weight, readied his hands, and watched them warily. The darkness of the cowls made it difficult not to be intimidated. One of those apes, unarmed, would be a pretty tough project, he judged; three or four of them with those neon quarterstaffs—bad news.

Flynn cocked his fists, despite a determination to employ all diplomacy. *Nothing left but grace under fire,* he sighed to himself.

One of the gorillas stepped forward without warning and bashed the disoriented Flynn in the arm with his staff. There was a dazzle of light, and agonizing pain rocketed from Flynn's fingertips to his shoulder. He fell back with a yelp, and knew that he was defenseless against such a weapon.

Those jokers were plainly not present for choir practice.

"Hey! Take it easy!" grated Flynn as they closed in around him. Maybe he really *was* lying in intensive care someplace with a concussion, but he didn't feel like dreaming about having his head handed to him. *Best keep it light,* he philosophized.

"Look, if this is about those parking tickets, I can explain everything!" But the Memory Guards of the Master Control Program, herding him toward the cells of the Training Complex, gave no indication of having heard him.

High over the Game Grid drifted the long, gleaming shape of Sark's Carrier, impregnable and vigilant and menacing, tacit threat and reminder. Recognizers came to and departed from its hangar bays without pause. Its free-standing antennae rotated in their fixed positions around its bridge, and its crew maintained constant surveillance. It was more than a vessel; it was the manifestation of Sark's—the MCP's—rule.

Sark himself, merciless Red Champion, stood within his podium gripping his energy handles, legs encased in the power outlets, consuming the energy allotted him by Master Control.

A crackle of static sounded briefly, then an image formed before him. It scintillated, rippling like disturbed water, then resolved into a visage Sark knew well, one that filled him with awe and carefully repressed dread.

The MCP's ghostly image hung before him, a burnished cylinder of lustrous metal. Its face rippled in multichrome pastels. Sark heard its voice pronounced loudly, making the bulkheads vibrate.

"SARK, ES—1117821. Open communication."

Sark's casque-helmeted head rose. "Yes, MCP," he responded, a little hoarsely, withdrawing his attention from the power intake. He squared his armored shoulders, waiting like a faithful, ferocious dog for the orders, the approval or punishment, that his master might care to mete out.

"I've a challenge for you, Sark." The MCP's voice was like death itself. "A new recruit. He's a tough case, but I want him treated in the usual manner. Train him for the games, let him hope for a while, and blow him away."

Sark relaxed the merest bit. Easy enough assignment; he'd

done precisely the same to so many programs that he'd lost track of them. And Sark had, with the orchestration of most of the MCP's resources, captured Tron. Maybe he was about to meet one of those Department of Defense programs; Sark relished the prospect of a contest with a truly antagonistic program. And that program would, indeed, eventually be destroyed.

A feral smile curved his lips. "You've got it. I've been hoping you'd send me somebody with a little moxie. What kind of program is he?"

"He's not any kind of program, Sark," the MCP answered with no flicker of emotion. "He's a User."

Sark nearly lost hold of the energy grips, dumbfounded. "A User?" he echoed, lowering his voice unconsciously in some remnant of worship, a shadow of reverence.

"That's right," Master Control answered with what sounded like an element of irritation at Sark's reaction. "He *pushed* me, in the Other World. When somebody pushes me, I push back. So I brought him down here."

Sark felt its scrutiny upon him. "What's the matter, Sark?" it asked, as he coped with the concept of deicide. "You look nervous."

Sark licked his lips. "Well, I—it's just—I don't know. A User. I mean . . ." He who had persecuted and destroyed so many programs who'd still believed in their Users, who'd been given by Master Control the task of eradicating that loyalty, could not now deny to himself an awe of the Users. He himself had never been able to expunge it, and suspected, though he would never have voiced it, that he shared it with the MCP. "Users wrote us. A User even wrote you."

"NO ONE USER WROTE ME!" the MCP stormed, and the Carrier quaked. Sark shrank from that anger. "I'm worth *millions* of their man-years!" It was a warning so plain that Sark dared not pursue that subject any further.

"But, what if I can't—" he labored.

"You'd rather take your chances with me?" Somewhere, the MCP altered the flow of energy. "You want me to slow down your power cycles for you?"

Sark the Champion felt the influx of power ebb, felt his own energy level plummet alarmingly. The eddy-currents of energy around the podium's sockets faded as the power fled from him. He slumped weakly, clutching the handgrips for support. Within him a terrible emptiness rose, debilitating and not to be defied, reminder of who was servant, and who master.

"Wait," he gasped. "I need that." Humbled, deprived of the strength Master Control allowed him, he saw that total obedience or total obliteration were his only options. Without Master Control he was not Champion, nor Command Program, nor even Warrior. The MCP misered its power jealously, and would accept the service only of those who obeyed it without question and without hesitation. And for Sark, existence was pointless without the high rank conferred upon him by Master Control. He'd drunk too deeply of power.

"Then, pull yourself together," Master Control ordered with nothing but severity in its tone. "Get this clown trained. I want him in the games until he dies playing. Acknowledge."

"Yes," Sark managed, clinging to his podium, chastised. "Acknowledged, Master Control."

The MCP watched him for another moment, and the Red Champion could feel its scorn. It was reassured once more that it, and it alone, held sway in the System.

And soon it would be so in that Other World; the Users would learn! "End of line," Master Control announced, and its projection disappeared.

Energy surged; Sark felt it rush through him, revitalizing, filling every part of him with strength and life. And still it came, swelling him until it seemed to radiate from him, lifting and exalting him. Sark threw back his helmeted head and drank it in, glorying in it. If bending knee to the MCP was the price of such indescribable power, he told himself as he rode the exultation, then it was a bargain with which he was content.

Flynn was being escorted down a long corridor, past door after door. The nearness of the doors to one another suggested very small rooms; he had a stomach-wrenching feeling that he knew what they were.

The two guards in front of him stopped by one of the doors and it opened to some mechanism or command he couldn't detect. Flynn hung back, hoping against hope that the cramped space within wasn't meant for him. One of the guards said, "Video Game Unit #18. In here, program."

Flynn's temper got the better of him. He reached for the guard, snarling, "Who you callin' 'program,' program?" But the guard grabbed Kevin Flynn with overwhelming strength while his fellow brandished a staff threateningly, and hurled Flynn into the cell.

The universe whirled around him while Flynn fought to recover physical and mental balance. The notion of simply ignoring it all, of trying to wake up or wait things out, wouldn't do. He'd felt pain when the guards had roughed him up, and time seemed to be passing at a realistic rate; events would continue, he was convinced, whether he wanted them to or not.

He leaned against the door, looking down at his hands. They glowed and pulsed. He was willing to bet that he was no longer seeing in the 3700-to-7000-angstrom range, and wasn't particularly eager to think about the rest of his bodily functions. A hardware phrase occurred to him: "User-friendly." *I bet* this *joint isn't,* he thought. He looked up from his hands, eyes wide. A tentative conclusion came to him, awful in its implications.

He forced himself to confront the things he'd heard and seen and felt, without self-deception. If reality was the product of mind—if awareness shaped existence—then, might not other intelligences fashion other worlds? *Reality's a matter of opinion,* Flynn's mind pounded at him. *We're all wave fronts on this bus.* He recalled Lora and Gibbs's experiment, and had a feeling he knew what had happened. He thrust those preoccupations aside, freeing his mind to deal with problems at hand.

Flynn turned and addressed himself to the fiendishly designed cell, and found no relief. It was cramped, allowing no comfort and providing little room, and had a transparent ceiling, undoubtedly for the convenience of guards. He'd never been fond of single-room occupancy.

Flynn's attention was drawn by low voices; he spied an opening to an adjoining cell, wherein a figure leaned in conversation with the prisoner in the next cell along. He couldn't make them out too clearly except to note that they shared his luminescent appearance.

Ram, glancing over his shoulder at Flynn, murmured to Tron, "New guy," and sized him up.

Tron shook his head in regret. "Another free program off the line." How many more, he wondered, would it take to put the entire System under the MCP and stamp out faith in the Users?

Ram sighed. "You really think the Users are still there?" He had put a note of doubt in it that alarmed Tron; if Ram wavered in his loyalty, who might not?

Tron was drained by constant rounds of competition in the arena and the confinement, which permitted no real rest. And he had thought, often, of the one he missed most, of she who meant everything to him. Not freedom, not survival, meant more than seeing Yori once more. At times, it seemed, his faith had come near failure. What was the point of it, what did it matter? MCP promised to take over the System without any real opposition but Tron's. Why hadn't the Users intervened? But then, Tron knew, they had—*he* was their instrument. But the cause, to set things right and restore order and purpose and safety to the System, seemed lost. Instead, there would be the dictatorship of Master Control Program and the savage spectacles of the beast Sark.

But, as always, another thought surfaced. Why would Sark and the MCP be so determined to stamp out loyalty to the Users if that loyalty didn't threaten them? The Command Program and the MCP were the fanatics, not the User-Believers; their brutal efforts to suppress belief in the Users only served to confirm convictions vital to Tron. As they increased their oppression, so they reinforced his faith.

"They'd better be," he answered Ram. "I don't want to bust out of here and find nothing but a lot of cold circuits waiting for me." And *Yori!* his mind resounded, the most elemental of prayers.

Ram smiled at Tron's comment; wordlessly, they sealed the agreement that there would be no bowing to Sark and Master Control, and that there would be a future.

Flynn, at his window, strained to make out his fellow prisoners more clearly. "Hey!" They turned to him in the dimness. He made to reach through the opening. "Who are you guys?"

As his hand came into the area framed by the opening,

it was stopped by something he couldn't see. Discharges leaped outward from his fingers; a bolt of pain/heat/cold coursed up his arm. He snatched his hand back in shock, jaw dropping. *"Youch!"*

One of the figures turned, and Flynn could see him more clearly. "You want to watch those force fields," Ram said. Flynn couldn't have been more in agreement.

He came over to Flynn, a figure of radiant colors, gray predominating, limned with the circuitlike lines, resembling some celestial being. He wore armor and helmet, as did Flynn, but not the half-tunic, half-sash overgarment. "You'll have plenty of chances to get hurt; don't worry about that."

Flynn chose to ignore the remark. But the implications of it made him feel as if the floor had just swung away from beneath him. He attempted to get a handle on things in Flynnish fashion: "Look, just so I can tell my friends what this dream was about—okay?—where *am* I?"

Ram regarded him strangely; he'd never seen a program quite like this stranger, never heard one speak this way. *Perhaps he's glitched,* decided Ram, who replied, "You're a . . . *guest,* of the Master Control Program."

Without a paddle, Flynn's mind said in no jocular manner. His sense of the absurd had long since given up the effort to convince him that it was time to wake up. But mention of the MCP summoned memories of himself at the console in the basement of ENCOM. He reached the inescapable conclusion that his situation was neither dream nor hallucination.

"They're going to make you play videogames," Ram finished. *I'm putting you on the Game Grid,* the MCP had promised Flynn, he remembered now.

He was relieved by Ram's words, though. "Well, great! That's no sweat. I play videogames better than *anybody*." He speculated on what the local record for *Space Paranoids* might be. Ram looked at him skeptically, but Flynn barely noticed. This whole loony setup might have its appeal. If the locals—whoever and whatever they were—set store by the ability to play videogames, Flynn figured, he might have himself a political career.

Further conversation was prevented by a heavy pounding noise, as the door to Flynn's cell opened. He looked up, to the origin of the pounding. A guard stood on the sheet of transparent material that was the ceiling of his cell; the ferrule of a staff struck against it once more. The guard moved on, pausing over Ram's cell, and Tron's, to pound on them.

Flynn, seeing no point in resisting, made his way into the corridor. Guards pulled other captives from their confinement up and down the row. He was shoved off in the desired direction but stopped suddenly, whirling on the cowled guard. "There's been a mistake! I gotta see the guy in charge!" If they thought they had to keep him in a cage just to get him to play videogames, he'd straighten that out fast. Bring on *Battle Zone!*

The hulking guard, and another, marched Flynn on his way once more. "You will," promised the one whom Flynn had addressed. Flynn liked the tone of it not in the least.

He was marched in a column of prisoners like himself, all wearing the half-tunic, onto a broad, terracelike area. He saw that he was in a complex reaching down and down, reminding him of an enormous strip-mining operation. Flynn gazed down into a circular pit, far below. The diameter of the place, he calculated, was a mile or more. *On this scale,* he reminded himself, *whatever that might mean.* It was sub-divided into areas modified for different uses, the floor of each graphed in squares of varying sizes. The arenas' walls were sheer, but above them rose level after level of expansive balconies, terraces, stages, and vantage points. Tiny figures moved about on many of them, allowing Flynn to gauge its size. He could think of no other structure so huge; it was as if the Grand Canyon had been executed in strange contours composed of geometric shapes and strips and patches of light. His astonishment almost made him stumble; he shuffled to avoid a collision with the program behind him.

The file of prisoners marched past another group of pro-grams, armored and gleaming in red, who wore disks affixed to their backs. None of them wore tunics, leading Flynn to believe that the garment was some sort of badge for neo-phytes. The red looked mean and contemptuous; as Flynn and the rest passed by, they called out insults and provoca-tions. Flynn gave them a hard look and hoped he'd get to shoulder up to a *Tail Gunner* against one of them with the others looking on. Under the circumstances, it was all he could. He trudged behind the others out into an open area, and stopped to the guard's command.

He'd seen no one who appeared to rank above the guards, and knew by now that talking to them was useless. But here, perhaps, he'd have a chance to get to someone with real pull and explain things. A guard stood on a rostrum overlooking the line of captives.

He exhorted them with an uplifted staff. "Look operative, you guys! Command Program Sark will explain the training procedures."

Flynn peered around expectantly, waiting for the opportunity to buttonhole somebody and get a few words in.

A shadow fell over the complex. For the first time, Flynn looked up. Again, his mouth hung open.

The sky of this strangest of all worlds was a fantastic vision, filled with brightness, and remarkable shapes and forms in unfathomable patterns, which reminded him somehow of clouds but resembled them little. He paid them scant attention though, when he saw what had blocked out the light. The craft was colossal, larger than the largest nuclear supercarrier, menacing in a cold, impervious way. Smaller shapes—though they would be large from close-up, Flynn saw—entered and left the vessel endlessly, swooping on missions or patrols.

Squinting for a better look, he gave a start of surprise. *Recognizers!* But not the tiny computer simulations he himself had conceived; those monsters were the size of the Arc de Triomphe! Flynn considered, with a certain tightness in his throat, what mention of "games" might truly imply.

Sark glared down disdainfully from on high, at the specks who were his new conscripts, and spoke, his words amplified so that the entire Game Grid heard him. "Greetings." Sarcasm dripped from the word. "The Master Control Program has chosen you to serve your System on the Game Grid."

The phrase now filled Flynn with apprehension as he considered the arena below. The chilling voice boomed from the sky again. "Those of you who continue to profess a belief in the Users will receive the standard substandard training. This will result in your eventual elimination."

The voice was without compassion—indeed, its owner plainly enjoyed the opportunity to toy with helpless victims. *What have I gotten myself into?* Flynn exclaimed to himself. Here were programs, their intelligence structuring a palpable World, and a power faction attempting to cut off all relationships with the Users, the better to rule. They'd hit on a pretty effective method, was Flynn's opinion. He mentally kicked himself for strolling into ENCOM so casually and putting himself right where the MCP could tackle him on its own ground.

That diabolical voice spoke on. "Those of you who renounce this superstitious and hysterical belief will be eligible to join the Warrior Elite of the MCP."

Two of the Reds standing behind the group laughed and nudged one another. The hard looks they gave the conscripts were clear enough; they had no preferences, and looked forward to combat or alliance with equal enthusiasm. They seemed bigger, more powerful than the prisoners, and Flynn assumed that to be by the MCP's design. And Flynn knew, too, that he would never be one of them; the option offered the others did not apply to him. The MCP was out for revenge.

The programs around him were muttering to one another about Sark's last remark. How could they yield their belief in the Users, they asked each other. How could they proclaim that they, and the System, were without any purpose or meaning but the MCP's? And that only left one alternative, in Sark's cold equation.

Flynn, gazing up at the enormous aircraft, forgot, for a moment, to be afraid. *Even here,* he thought, *the old, old evil: surrender your beliefs or surrender your life.*

Sark leaned forward on the bridge of his Carrier, to study the insects below. It was a comfort to him that the captive User was indistinguishable from the others. He thrust aside doubts, and thoughts of colossal, shining beings who'd shaped and directed the System in times past. The User was, after all, no great issue.

He finished, "You will each receive an identity disk. Everything you do or learn will be imprinted on this disk. If you lose your disk or fail to follow commands, you will be subject to immediate de-resolution. That is all."

Now all the conscripts were directed to look down into the arena. Flynn saw that, far below, a game—*a duel,* he corrected himself—was about to begin. Arrayed against a lone conscript were four of the Red Warrior Elite. Sparkling, spinning circles of light flashed and flew between them, and Flynn, recalling Sark's mention of disks, watched in fascination.

Not that it's likely to do you much good, he thought regarding the unfortunate program who fought alone, *but I'm for you. Believe what you want to believe! Get 'em!*

Chapter Seven

TRON HELD HIS disk lightly, his weight forward on the balls of his feet, and met the gaze of his enemies.

They tried their best to show him nothing but ferocity, but none of them could conceal a degree of doubt. This was no hapless accounting program they faced; the very fact that there were four of them against him was proof of that.

And, they all knew the reputation of Tron, the independent, the User-Believer. By recanting his belief, Tron could have earned himself high rank, perhaps become the equal of Sark, or even supplanted him. In the minds of the four Reds, Tron knew by now, would be the same thought: if they'd had his prowess, they wouldn't have wasted it defending their beliefs. That was a vast irony to him; they would never understand how his convictions and his abilities were intertwined.

Two Warriors went into casting positions. "Go," one called. From that crouch they released, with snapping, side-on casts. The disks came, one low, one high. Tron went into a defensive posture, his own disk held before him in both hands, vertically, one leg set behind him now for balance. Calculating angles and speeds, he saw nothing else, thought of nothing else, but the weapons racing toward him.

70

He deflected the first with a crash of discharging energy, and it wobbled away, spent. But he had no time to watch it, and lowered his disk instantly to deflect the second. That one, too, rebounded from Tron's disk. He launched a quick counterattack, throwing at one of the now unarmed Reds. His disk caught the Red, opening a wound in him, with a corona burst. The wound roiled with escaping energy, showing signs of de-rezzing.

Flynn looked on, amazed; it was a far cry from his arcade. And that User-Believer! Flynn could only admire the sure, quick movements, the complete control and unthinking agility.

Another conscript, seeing his expression, indicated the lone combatant. "See that Warrior? One hundred and ten wins, no losses."

Flynn nodded, not doubting it a bit. But all the duelists had their disks back now, and the four Reds, the wounded one included, were circling their enemy. As much as Flynn admired the User-Believer's skill, he didn't see how the program could win.

Far down on the arena floor, one of the Elite yelled, "Waste him!" Crouched, expectant, nerves thrumming, Tron waited. All four hurled their disks at the same moment.

Tron ducked, dodged to one side, and blocked one disk with his own. The others passed through the air where he'd been standing a moment before. Tron instantly threw, and struck a Red Warrior who screamed as he was hit. The Red de-rezzed in a searing release of energy as the aura of Tron's weapon spread over him, replacing his own red one.

Tron straightened, took his disk as it returned to him. Holding it in a practiced attack grip, he pivoted, and cast. The Red who was his target saw, tried to elude the whirling plate of light, but failed. Struck, he crumpled backward; the shimmering scan lines and crackling static of his own de-rezzing were the last things he saw and heard. Tron ducked a second cast from another Red, throwing himself flat and rolling to his feet, rising just in time to leap out of the way as a low-flying disk sought him.

He caught his own disk as it returned, recovered, and cast once more in midair. The weapon found another Red who, not expecting such blinding speed even from the storied Tron, could only stare with foolish shock on his face as he was hit and a boiling de-rezzing engulfed him. The other Reds became grimmer, and fear showed on their faces. The odds were far different now and their adversary much, much more than they'd expected him to be.

Tron addressed himself calmly to the remaining Reds, keeping himself from any overhasty move, reminding himself that great caution was still imperative—was always so, on the Game Grid. His disk returned to his hand like a thing alive. He took a step and hurled it again, with all the power of his arm behind it.

The Elite at whom he'd thrown held up his own weapon to block, but Tron's crashed through it with a violent meeting of energies and burst against the startled Red. Like a triumphant nova, the blazing aura of Tron's disk spread to envelop the Red as he de-rezzed.

A stillness descended over the arena as Tron and his remaining opponent confronted each other. The Red had lost control of his fear now, and could only watch Tron with bulging eyes. Then, slowly, he brought his disk up, readying against all hope to hurl again. Tron saw that, as always, there could be no end when Elite and User-Believer entered an arena but for one side or the other to be de-rezzed. He cast once more, eager for it to be finished.

The last Red wailed as the radiance of Tron's disk enfolded him.

Tron stretched forth his hand and his disk came to it obediently. He stood alone, panting slightly now that the battle was over, knowing that User-Believers and Reds alike were gazing down on him, letting the combat speak for itself. A part of him wondered bitterly what the next challenge would be and, if he survived, the next after that.

Flynn, staring down, asked the conscript who'd spoken to him, "Who *is* that guy?"

The program's face grew animated. "That's Tron. He fights for the Users." There was tremendous pride to it; Tron was the only one to whom these downtrodden, terrorized captives could look for hope and vindication.

"Tron?" Flynn echoed, recalling Alan's project. That explained a lot, including Tron's ability to cope so graphically with the Reds, and the obvious determination of Sark and the MCP to see him humbled and destroyed. Tron might be the key to the whole problem.

"Silence!" bellowed one of the guards as Flynn was about to follow up with a dozen more questions. "No communicating!"

Flynn shut up hastily, having no wish to test the punishments of the Training Complex. Overhead, Sark's Carrier swung off on a new course, now that his entertainment was over.

Within the ship, in the heady embrace of the podium, Sark glanced out from the command bridge. At his side, a lieutenant of the Elite waited nervously. Sark, drinking in the energy allocated him by the MCP, asked, "Which conscript just won that disk match?"

"That one's name is Tron," answered the other. "He's a fanatic User-Believer, a troublemaker."

Sark's face twisted with distaste, the news spoiling the sublime pleasure of energy absorption. *"Tron."* His lips curled at the name. "Isn't he dead yet? You're going to have to increase the odds." Tron would be easy enough to get rid of, Sark thought, but that was entirely beside the point. Executing him wouldn't suffice; Tron must be *defeated.*

Back in his cell, Flynn tried once more to find some small measure of comfort, pacing a short path back and forth, trying to fit together all the astounding things he'd learned since he'd come to the chimerical counterreality. He'd just completed an exhausting training session, but his mind was still going full choke.

He'd lost count of the number of drill periods he'd spent with the disk or power-cesta, or riding a light-cycle. The training had been, as advertised, substandard. Most of the captive programs held little hope of survival in the arena. But Flynn had discovered in himself a certain talent for the games—understandably, since he'd invented many of them, and based them on skills or sports with which he'd been familiar. He'd picked up techniques and tricks with surprising speed; his strong competitive nature had been his most important asset. There was a tremendous difference between playing a game via buttons and controls and ducking a combat disk, but he'd made of himself a promising Warrior trainee. He hadn't been surprised when no one had asked him to recant his faith in the Users.

Ram, in the next cell, was holding his disk up, edge-on, examining it closely for any imperfections. He was whistling an eerie, lilting tune that Flynn didn't recognize as any User music. Flynn drifted over that way; he'd had little time to talk to Ram and none at all to speak to the next prisoner along. Their schedules of practice and the timing of the combats in which the other two had participated since Flynn's arrival had had them out of their cells and in different places at different times.

But Flynn had learned one thing. The name of that other program was Tron.

Now he edged up to the opening between the cells, automatically careful to avoid another run-in with its defensive field. Ram continued his whistling, lost in thought. *Just like any other guy you'd run into,* mused Flynn, *except that he's a program. Wonder if I'll ever get used to that?*

"Hey, Ram," he called. The music broke off in midnote, and Ram looked around at him. "What were you . . . y'know, before?"

Ram brightened, plainly to memories that cheered him. "Oh, I was an actuarial program; worked at a big insurance company. It really gives you a great feeling, helping folks plan for their future needs."

He'd half-lapsed into a fond reverie. Flynn, who'd only intended to draw him out in order to learn more about Tron, felt a little guilty. A passing thought occurred to him; what would Dr. Gibbs think if he could see how very much useful function meant to these programs?

"And of course," Ram was saying, "if you look at the payments as an annuity, over the years, the cost is really—"

Flynn could bear no more. "Yeah, yeah; that's great."

Ram, not noticing how little enthusiasm Flynn was showing, countered politely, "How about yourself?"

A question Flynn had been expecting with some misgiving. The truth would have the programs treating him as if he were demented, at best. At worst . . . a heretic? In any case, there was absolutely no way he could prove his story and it could only confuse matters at this point. "Oh, I don't remember too much. Name's Flynn."

Ram nodded sagely. "Sure, a little disorientation. That's normal, when they transport you. It'll come back to you."

Thinking how much *he* would like to come back to *it* instead, Flynn went on, "Where's your friend Tron? I gotta talk to—"

He was stopped by shouts from above and the peremptory hammering of guards' staff butts on the ceiling overhead. Flynn looked up at them, then at Ram, who was silent. No more conversation now; somehow Flynn sensed that it was no training session to which he would be taken this time.

Marching down the corridor between the guards, he tried his best to quiet his stomach and concentrate on what lay ahead. "You guys sure are friendly," he told the darkened cowls of the guards with elaborately false warmth. They gave no sign of having heard him.

From the bridge of his Carrier, Sark watched the monitor screen, evaluating the User's reaction—or lack of it—to the upcoming match. The User had shown unusual talent during the training process, and so that training had been terminated. Now, being led to the Game Grid, Flynn exhibited behavior no different from that of thousands of Warriors Sark had seen, though the Command Program was, as always, too high above the complex to see facial features in any detail. But this User seemed interchangeable with the programs he and his kind had created. Sark drew reassurance from that.

Command Program Sark spoke over his shoulder: "Wait. Let him fight one of his own kind." The order was relayed to select a User-Believer as adversary. Sark smiled, wishing that he *could* pit two Users against each other and regretting that he himself couldn't be the one to destroy a User.

Flynn, nervously adjusting his half-tunic, walked with his guards out onto a broad ledge overlooking the Game Grid. From it, a bridge of solid force stretched to the concentric rings of the jai alai game. Beside him was another program who'd been brought forth, a conscript whose name, Flynn recalled, was Crom. Each of them now wore an electronic cesta over his right hand. Flynn was confused, peering around for the Red Warriors he expected to meet in combat; he saw only the pudgy Crom.

Crom, without hesitation, walked one bridge and took up his place on a ring there. Flynn gave the guards a perplexed look, but they only stared at him wordlessly. With an inward shrug, he walked the second bridge and waited uneasily. Then both bridges disappeared.

Flynn and Crom gazed at one another across the gulf. Flynn essayed a grin. "Looks like we're in the same boat, here—"

Crom, nervous, glaring with resentment and fear, shouted, "You think you're gonna wipe me out, don't you?" He knew of the aptitude Flynn had shown at practice and he presumed that Flynn was aware of what was about to happen and welcomed it. Crom could think of no other reason for being pitted against another conscript; his antagonist must have agreed to join the Elite, and slay Crom as proof of his conversion.

Comprehension was forming in Flynn's mind as he watched the look on Crom's face. "No, I—"

Without waiting to hear, Crom fired the blazing game-ball up at the mirror with his cesta. It rebounded from the mirror and sped at Flynn's rings. Flynn jumped, cesta out, intending to intercept it, but misjudged angles and distances. The game-ball struck the ring just ahead of him, dissolving it. Crom cackled with delight.

Flynn skidded to a stop with a wild windmilling of arms, barely retaining his balance and avoiding the long plunge to the grid floor below. He was staring down in horror when he heard a sound from above. Another pellet hit the mirror, aimed straight at him.

Reflexes cut in before he had time to doubt. He ducked, bringing up the glowing, humming cesta. He caught the glowing ball cleanly, brought the cesta around and tossed it back at the mirror with smooth precision, without hesitation or debate. The pellet struck the mirror and rebounded from it with no reduction in speed or energy. Crom, wild-eyed, tried to gauge the sizzling ricochet. He dove, missed, plowed to a stop. The pellet released its charge on contact with one of his rings, and the ring de-rezzed in a spectacular display.

Flynn threw up an arm, elated. "Okay!" He'd expected to go up against a Red Warrior but, seeing himself matched against Crom, presumed that this was some sort of advanced training or graduation exercise and that both conscripts would be preserved for the real thing.

Overhead, Sark watched and gloated. Either the User would die at the hands of a User-Believer or a User-Believer would be destroyed by a User. Sark savored the irony, and knew that the duel would stand as an example to the other conscripts, of the importance of self-preservation.

Back in their cells, Ram and Tron continued the quiet conversation they'd carried on throughout their captivity, relaxing as best they could, backs to the common window. Their quiet, solemn talks were in sharp contrast to the merciless drill and combat of the Game Grid. Ram had come to draw great encouragement from Tron, from his loyalty to the Users. And there was Tron's straightforward reasoning: why, indeed, would Sark and the MCP militate so viciously against User-Believers if their beliefs didn't present some threat?

When he'd thought it through, Ram had finally decided that the demonstrations of power, the taking of conscripts, were a keystone to Master Control's authority. If MCP and Sark could get programs to deny the existence of Users in contradiction to what all programs knew to be true, what then might they *not* order programs to do? The entire System, and the power to reshape it, would lie within their grasp.

"That new guy was asking about you," Ram said quietly.

From the half-lit cell beyond, Tron's measured voice answered, "Too bad he's in a match now. I'll probably never meet him."

"You might," Ram replied. "There's something different about him." He couldn't quite find the words for it, that odd acuity and irreverence of Flynn's, that air about him that he knew far more than he would tell. But Ram sensed that Flynn was no ordinary program, that they'd be seeing him again.

High over the Grid, Flynn pounced on Crom's next throw, a long reach. The compound-interest program's casts were becoming less and less effective as his desperation grew and his rings vanished before Flynn's attacks. Now, Flynn bagged the shot, recovered, then pitched the game-ball back at the mirror.

The light-node bounced off the mirror and scored on one of Crom's remaining rings. The ring disappeared in a nimbus of energy as Crom bounded to one of his last remaining circles. The cast now went to Flynn; he weighed the crackling game-ball waiting in his cesta. He drew back for a cast, intending to knock out another of Crom's rings, but then saw the look of dismay and resignation on the program's face, and relented.

With a quick glance to the hovering Carrier, Flynn laughed. "Here's an easy one!"

He lifted the pellet upward; it glanced off the reflective surface and came straight at Crom; an easy one, as promised. Crom, poised to meet it, was filled with uncertainty. This new Warrior was good, and sure of himself, giving up an advantage like this—if he was to be trusted—even though Crom had done his best to send Flynn down in defeat. That meant, Crom decided, that this giveaway must be a trick. Crom wavered; at the last instant, he saw that Flynn had done as he'd said he would.

Crom's best wasn't adequate; he missed the ball and it crashed into the ring on which he was standing. Crom, who'd seen that he had no hope of making the catch, threw himself toward his innermost ring, his last, with a frantic thrashing of arms and legs, just as the one beneath him de-rezzed.

Crom just managed to catch hold of the remaining ring with hand and power-cesta. There he hung, feet kicking, high over the Grid. Flynn waited for Crom to haul himself up. Sark, in his Carrier, frowned at the monitor screen, furious with this unforgivable compassion. Such demonstrations could destroy the motivation of his Warriors, ruining all that he'd worked for, contaminating User-Believer and Elite alike.

Flynn gazed across at frightened, weary Crom. The program was still kicking, scrambling hopelessly to draw himself up onto his ring, waiting dully for what he presumed would be the final shot of the game. Flynn saw now that no one was going to intervene; the game was supposed to proceed to its conclusion, with Crom dropping like a maimed bird and de-rezzing on the Grid below.

Flynn had no intention of winning any game that way. Staring at Crom's face, he tried to tell himself that the program was nothing but a collection of algorithms, but he wasn't buying it, not when he saw Crom's expression. Crom, seeing that Flynn hesitated to make the cast, could hardly have regarded him with greater disbelief if he'd known who Flynn really was.

A voice reverberated above them, drawing their glances: "FINISH THE GAME!" Sark commanded.

There, like an evil vision in a dream, the Command Program's face filled the mirror. Flynn's breath caught as he saw the projection. Despite the grotesque flarings and design of the casque, and the interplay of energies and colors, that face was Edward Dillinger's.

Flynn gritted his teeth, staring upward. This answered a lot of questions, but raised even more. But the image of Dillinger/Sark decided him, once and for all, on which side he stood in the System's struggle.

As Crom waited to perish, Flynn balled his fist, filled lungs, compressed lips, and shouted his reply to the loathsome face above: *"No!"*

Elsewhere, the refusal had its effect. Over the sounds of the bus station, one of the kids, stabbing at lifeless firing buttons and pulling uselessly at a control grip, complained, "What's wrong with it?"

The videogame remained as before, still alight, but all play had halted. Nothing he could do elicited any further action. The other player, a classmate, answered, "I don't know; on the blink, or somethin'. Damn!"

Angered by the interruption, they hit the controls and banged the machine with the heels of their hands.

Flynn, head lowered, ignored the command that beat at his ears from the Carrier: "KILL HIM!"

Kill . . . Flynn held up the cesta, contemplating it gravely. Perhaps, he thought, convictions were the only things that passed undistorted through the weird translation to the Electronic World. It might be a conceit, but he was ready to believe that wrong and right were constants.

Flynn turned the power-cesta over, letting the game-ball drop harmlessly toward the Grid. He drew a deep breath, then smirked up at Sark's enraged face. "You'll regret this," the image promised. Crom looked stunned.

Flynn laughed aloud. *Now what're you gonna do, El Supremo? Gonna kill me, the winner? You could run real short of converts that way!*

A moment later, his vast satisfaction left him. By some unseen command, Crom's last ring began to de-rezz. Crom still hung from it, feet churning, helpless. Hope had come back into his face with Flynn's refusal, but now his features twisted in utter defeat, his doom having found him after all.

Flynn, unable to help, could only look on. With a last cry as the ring lost all substance, Crom plummeted, tumbling toward the Grid floor, watched by both Flynn and Sark.

Sark's finger poised by a button on the Carrier's bridge, one that would send the User to an identical fate. Despite the MCP's order that Flynn was to meet his end in combat, Sark thought it would be safer to be rid of him immediately. The User was too unpredictable, too independent, unconstrained by any of the fundamental presumptions under which programs thought and acted.

Sark's hand wavered over the control as he strained to commit an act in direct disobedience of the will of the MCP. The finger shook as the Command Program fought an almost physical battle to follow his own will. But it was, in the end, no use; teeth locked, he resigned himself once more to the knowledge that he was the MCP's to command, with no possibility of defiance.

And as Sark snatched his hand away, the voice of Master Control was abruptly all around him. "He is to die in the games!"

Flynn was glaring up at the mirror with impotent rage. The face was gone from it now and Flynn, expecting some further contest of wills or a renewal of combat, was surprised to see his bridge reappear. Two guards double-timed across it to take him away once more. Still, he had the feeling that things were about to get worse.

Chapter Eight

ON THE WAY out of the jai alai area, Flynn was bumped by a pair of husky Elite Warriors, a deliberate jostling. The guards pretended not to notice. One of the Reds whirled on him, snarling, "Outta my way, rookie!"

Flynn thought of the four Reds who'd ganged up on Tron, and of the pitiless murder of poor little Crom. He decided that, while he wouldn't slay User-Believers just to save his own skin, he had nothing against taking on the Elite. One supple sequence of movements had his disk in his hand; his eyes invited the other to do the same.

"Out of *my* way, zero-bit," said Flynn quietly.

The Red met his stare for a moment, then backed away. "Sure, sure; just kiddin'." His companion seized him by the arm and pulled him away as Flynn gradually relaxed, watching them go. He replaced his disk on his back, and the guards fell in with him again.

It wasn't long before he realized that he wasn't being taken to his cell. Understanding now that his captors meant to toss him into one mortal duel after another until he lost, he cudgeled his brain for something to do about it. But he could think of nothing, aside from making it a costly project for Sark and the ranks of the Elite.

81

His preoccupation was cut short as he was escorted into the holding area for the light-cycle contest. There, he found two User-Believers already waiting. He recognized the closest, Ram, even as he went to take his place with them.

Ram's face broke into a surprised look, then a delighted smile. "Flynn!" He turned to his companion. "Look, Tron; he survived!"

Flynn glanced sharply to the other User-Believer as he passed Ram, curious about the legendary User Champion. A tall figure stood there; Flynn got his first good look at Tron.

"Alan!" he exclaimed.

Tron frowned, disturbed by something he couldn't quite bring to mind, like a shadow from a dream. He examined the new program, then demanded, "Where did you hear that name?"

Flynn groped, confused, for an answer. He'd concluded for an instant that the MCP had zapped Alan as well as himself, but for some reason Alan didn't seem to recognize him. "Well, isn't that—"

"My User's name, yeah," Tron finished for him. "But how—"

"I, uh," Flynn fumbled, knowing now that this was no digitized man of the Other World. It came to him then that Tron had been in the System for a long time before he, Flynn, had shown up. Overcoming his initial shock, Flynn saw that this wasn't the time to go into his real origin. As he took his place next to Tron, he improvised, "I'm a program from a User that—that knows Alan." *Not too far from the truth,* he congratulated himself.

"He was disoriented in transport, Tron," Ram put in.

"Yeah," Flynn added out of the side of his mouth. "But I'm remembering all kinds of stuff. Like, my User wants me to go after the MCP." That put surprise on Tron's face; he was plainly impressed with Flynn.

But just then three Red Warriors entered; they were loud, rough, anxious for combat, slapping one another's shoulders and laughing harshly. They lined up opposite the User-Believer team, a few paces from them. The two teams eyed each other without comment. *Even odds,* Flynn reflected; *they must figure these Elite are good.*

They suddenly felt the coursing and crackling of transport beams passing through them. Both teams abruptly disappeared

n a haze of static, to reappear on the Grid, still facing each
ther, but separated now by a distance of a half-mile.

Sark's Carrier maintained position over the Game Grid,
directly above. High, polished walls enclosed the place, and
over it floated a number of Recognizers. The walls were
marked with giant numerals, strange ciphers, and symbols
unintelligible to Flynn, in varieties and combinations of
gleaming colors.

"That's what my User wants too," Tron told Flynn. Tron
was the answer to his dilemma, Flynn felt sure now. If
Flynn's efforts in the laser lab hadn't made it possible to
get the Tron program free of the MCP, maybe there was
something he could do here in the System.

A warning buzzer sounded; the race was about to start. "I
know," Flynn answered Tron. Tron and Ram looked at him
strangely, wondering how he knew the things he did. There'd
been little time to sort things out, but both programs found
themselves inclined to trust the peculiar newcomer.

Flynn, for his part, was finding Tron a revelation. He
brought much of Alan Bradley into sharp focus. Flynn saw
in Tron an absolute stubbornness when he felt he was right,
commitment to beliefs, determination to see that justice was
served.

The three leaned forward, each of them now gripping a
strangely designed set of handlebars. Light circled and swirled
around them, resolving itself, as their light-cycles were
brought into existence. Flynn held the posture as he'd been
taught, pulling his feet up as he felt the vehicle coalesce
under and around him. The cycles glowed with power; Tron's
in gold, Flynn's red, and Ram's green. Across the arena, the
Reds' cycles had also taken on substance, in blue.

The light-cycles were about nine feet from end to end,
two-wheeled, all aerodynamic curves and racing lines from
fairing to tail. Their rear wheels were of conventional design,
but the front ones were broad, nearly spherical. The rider's
back, once he was hunched down over his handlebars and
controls, became part of a smooth, nearly drag-free shape.
Flynn mentally reviewed the techniques and fine points of
the game, and he and the others revved their engines.

Somewhere above them, Sark touched a control stud. A
siren sounded across the arena; the race had begun.

All six cyclists gunned their machines and accelerated

away, tucked tightly within their cycles. From the rear of each vehicle, a spume of white force rose like the wake of a speedboat to solidify almost instantly into a partitioning wall coded to the color of the rider's team; blue for the Elite, each conscript in his individual hue.

Tron, the most experienced combatant, took the lead. Ram and Flynn veered off to the right and left, riding the grid lines of the arena floor precisely, as they must. Their turns were made nearly instantaneously at grid intersections. Off in the distance the Elite did the same, leaving one of their number to race head-on at Tron. The gap between them disappeared with harrowing speed. Tron watched his opposite number grow with his approach and fixed all his attention on his own vehicle and his enemy's.

Just as it seemed that the two light-cycles, inscribing their walls across the grid, must crash directly into each other, the two riders made lightning turns, Tron's left and the Elite Warrior's right, to run parallel to one another. Off they raced, throwing up barrier-wakes behind them in blue and gold.

In other parts of the arena the remaining four antagonists sped along, bringing more partitioning into being, turning abruptly and maneuvering for their lives as the arena began to fill with the cycles' mazes of light-walls.

Over Tron's communicator, Flynn's voice complimented that first head-on turn: "Nice one!" Tron and his opponent sped across the arena floor, neck and neck. Then began the perilous competition, each trying to box the other in, or get the other to turn at the wrong time and crash into a wall.

Tron's voice came back over the communicator: "Ram, stay all the way over!"

Ram peeled off from his course in response, the turn coming in an instant, acknowledging, "I've got control. Go ahead."

Tron and the Warrior against whom he was paired zoomed toward one of the clifflike walls that enclosed the arena. Tron maneuvered, and the Elite player found himself trapped between a gold partition and Tron's cycle, and the barrier it created as it roared along, a second wall of gold.

Tron's opponent couldn't slow or stop; once begun, the game was continued at speed. By keeping just ahead of him, Tron contained any effort that the Elite might make to turn, chuting him toward the arena wall. An instant later the Red's cycle crashed into it with such a tremendous liberation of energy as Warrior and cycle de-rezzed, that a segment of the arena wall itself also de-rezzed. Instantly, the wall that had been generated by the Elite Warrior faded from existence.

Flynn was alongside an opponent, bent low on the handlebars as the fairing's slipstream tore at him. He grinned into the blast; he'd always enjoyed motorcycles. The bike he rode now was superior to anything he'd ever ridden, its responses immediate, its speed breathtaking. No machine in that Other World could have duplicated its performance.

They made a turn together, swinging the balloonlike front tires in vector changes at the intersections of the grid lines. Flynn eluded impact with one of his antagonist's barriers, then another, and saw a third rise up directly before them both, all in moments. The arena had become a labyrinth where split-second decisions and constant attention were required to keep from colliding with something; the enemy's maneuvers were an unceasing threat. The need for turns grew more frequent as the teams sectioned and subsectioned the gridded floor. It was becoming impossible to tell whether another barrier or an open stretch lay around the next turn. Memory was some help, but the mazework thrown up behind the five remaining cycles was complicated and fast-growing, and there was little time to study it. Instinct and training and reflexes came to the fore.

Flynn avoided a second attempt by his opponent to kill him. He found himself screaming straight at the arena wall where the first Red Warrior had smashed up. The gap left by that impact had not yet rezzed back up; an opening in the wall remained, narrow and jagged-edged. Kevin Flynn, with no idea what might obstruct him in the gap, or what might lie beyond, nevertheless saw any opportunity for escape as a good one. The only certain way to die would be to remain prisoner in the Training Complex. Given that, Flynn was willing to risk just about anything, including the possibility of frying himself like a bug in another of those force fields.

"This is it!" he shouted into his communicator. Ram and Tron heard, but couldn't comprehend. "Come on!" Flynn urged, aiming for the opening, leaving a curtain of red light behind him as he went. An Elite swooped in at him for the kill, and Ram and Tron headed his way to see what his plan was.

The arena wall sped at Flynn and his enemy, the gap growing. The Red finally saw that Flynn had no intention of turning, and made a last-second attempt to save himself. But he'd waited too long, and hit the wall with terrific velocity just as Flynn shot the gap in the arena's side. The impact de-rezzed more of the wall.

Sark, watching from above, ranted, outraged. He'd thought to see the User perish in collision with the wall, ridding him of that problem for good. But this: *escape!* Unthinkable; unprecedented! Sark hammered a fist on the panel before him, calling down his Recognizers.

Below, Tron and Ram still dueled the remaining Red. Tron had seen Flynn's exit and been shocked by it. The MCP, he decided, must be hoarding more of the System's power than ever, so much so that even the re-rezzing of the Grid had been impaired. And, thrilling to the idea of freedom, he asked himself, *Why not?*

Ram had seen and heard too, and now he swung his machine hard, boxing the last Warrior, forcing him to hold a grid line. The Warrior hit a red barrier at full speed, evaporating in a caldronous de-rezzing.

Ram changed course, swung in parallel to Tron, and then they shot along side by side. "What do you think?" Ram asked over the communicator, terse with hope.

Tron knew exuberance, the chance to run freely and independently once more. "Do it!" he yelled into his mike. The pair made for the gap.

Sirens rent the air of the Training Complex. A gargantuan voice echoed across it, "WARRIORS MUST STAY WITHIN THEIR UNITS. REPEAT: ALL WARRIORS MUST STAY WITHIN THEIR UNITS. WARNING. WARNING." It became muted with distance as they ignored it and roared on.

Sark uttered a taut exclamation. The programs were emulating the User! His worst fears had been made real; not only had the User defied traditional constraints, but he'd gotten other programs to follow his lead. And worst of all, Tron was among them. Once more, Sark exhorted his Recognizers.

The Recos swooped in as Ram and Tron blurred toward the waiting gap. One descended on them with pincers together to form a huge pile driver. The pile driver slammed down just as the two shot the jagged opening, missing them by a hair'sbreadth, making the Grid shake. Then the Reco rose from the small opening to fly over the arena walls and resume the chase.

In a narrow conduit outside the arena, Ram and Tron caught up with Flynn, who'd slowed to wait for them. The force of the original de-rezzing had been channeled along the conduit; another zigzag notch at its far end gave them a way out. Here, outside the Grid, the light-cycles no longer threw up their barriers.

They emerged from the broached wall into an enormous corridor and set off at high speed. Aboard his Carrier, Sark lashed out, batting aside and flooring a guard who'd had the misfortune to be nearby. Overhead, a control overseer worked furiously in his monitoring bucket. Sark opened a general communications channel. "Get them!" he shrieked. "Send out every Game Tank on the Grid!" His choler peaked, in a bellow that threw fear into every program in the Complex. *"GET THEM!"*

The light-cycles emerged single file into an open area. Scores of depressions the size of city blocks were arranged in precise ranks and files to either side, divided by the squares of roadway. Two Recos swooped like hawks upon the fugitives, pincers spread wide to grasp or fire. The escapees raced for the resumption of the narrow corridor at the far end of the open area.

They did not reach it with any time to spare. The lead Reco slammed against the wall over them as they entered the little opening. As the first Reco rebounded, the second collided with it. The two machines hung there, stymied. Tron, Ram, and Flynn swept in tight formation through a long, narrow room, flanked on either side by rows of missiles poised on parked mobile launchers. In the next part of the vast arsenal, silent tanks waited, side by side to the right and left.

The tanks were dark, inactive, but not all were unmanned. As the fleeing conscripts raced along, vehicles to either side suddenly rezzed brighter and charged out at them. Tron and Flynn made it in a flash of yellow and orange, as the tanks' prows closed in on them. But Ram had to slew his cycle to the left to avoid one, then right to miss a second. He thought for an instant that he would die under the light-treads of a third, but made it by—without room to spare.

The tanks wheeled to pursue. The lead vehicle's gunner tracked them on his targeting scope, trying to bracket them for a shot. "Fire!" yelled the gunner. The long cannon spat its blinding chevron, but the round went wide. Three figures, hugged close to their cycles, sped out of his line of fire. "Missed," he gritted.

The trio raced down a ramp laid out in squares delineated by light. Salvos of tank cannonfire blossomed to the sides and behind them. The white V's of the cannonade sent rings of multichrome energy expanding from their impact. The escapees focused on their only possible salvation, high-speed flight. The sleek Game Tanks increased speed, raising commo with other contingents to try to block the way ahead. The unit leader relayed his situation report to Sark.

"Units exiting the Defensive Zone." There could be no more ambushes now; only pursuit.

Outside the Game Grid for the first time, Flynn found himself riding for his life through a fantastic landscape of glowing walls, modular shapes, and darting vector lines. He was not unhappy. The three sped past huge cipher panels and rows of gleaming, angular buttresses. A tank unit fell in behind, and the three rode at maximum speed, weaving back and forth and rounding turn after turn, leaning close to the floor-ground, denying the tankers a clear shot.

They flashed out onto a wide landing, a sort of turning bay at the brink of an overhang. Tron barely slid to a side-on stop, the half of one wheel of his gold light-cycle over the very edge of the landing. Hundreds of feet below was a gridded canyon floor. The turning bay overlooked a terrain of tremendous cylinders, piled megaforms, slotted towers, ledge-roadways, and stark bridgespans. The entire vista was luminous with the brilliant light surfaces and demarcations of the Electronic World.

The three immediately set off along the ledge-roadway, desperate to put distance between themselves and the war machines. "Target units accelerating!" the lead tank commander snapped, forcing more speed from his vehicle. One after another the Game Tanks plunged out onto the landing. The first, like Tron, just managed to halt on the edge of

Dillinger at his desk

Alan, Lora, and Flynn break into ENCOM

Lora leaves Flynn at her terminal

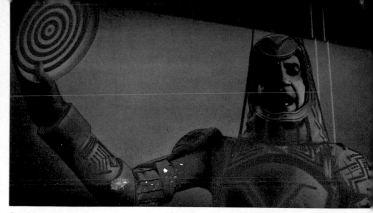

Sark

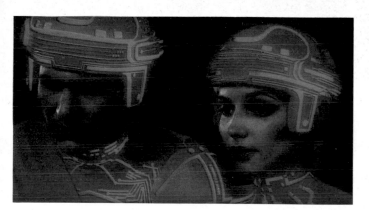

Flynn and Yori

Interior of the Tank with CLU at the controls

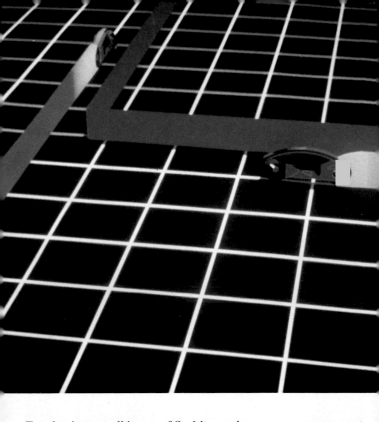

Tron begins to wall in one of Sark's warriors

Sark's warrior hits the wall and derezzes

Light cycles escaping from game grid

Approach to the MCP

the turning bay. But the tanks had crowded up too closely upon one another; their commanders had been determined to carry out Sark's orders, dreading what failure would earn them. The second tank smashed into the first, pushing it over the edge of the planiform cliff. The lead tank tumbled to the grid below, the programs within it screaming out the last moments of their lives. Then an angry blast of force took its place, and it was gone.

The three cycles howled in echelon along a curving ledge toward a division in a vast sweep of wall. Pursuit bogged down, the Game Tanks blocking one another as a new caution dampened the commander's inclination toward disorderly, full-speed chase.

Flynn accepted Tron's lead without question, and only hoped that the User Champion could find some place of safety where they might debate their next move.

They entered the division and descended a long downgrade, moving slowly in the murk. Among the twists and turns of the interior of the place, Tron found a final incline that ended in a cul-de-sac. The place reminded Flynn of a cavern, its walls and ceiling formed from blockish protrusions—trapezoids, squares, parallelograms. A soft blue light pervaded. Tron and Ram glided to a stop; Flynn followed suit.

Energy surged around them. In moments, the light-cycles had de-rezzed. Flynn only hoped that they'd be able to summon the bikes up again later; he couldn't shake the feeling that they'd be needing them. He stretched, took a deep breath.

"Oh, *man!* When you're on the other side of the screen, these games look so *easy!*"

Ram and Tron stared at Flynn, wondering if he'd lost his senses. Flynn reminded himself to speak more guardedly. But he saw that he'd have to tell his companions the truth before long. He'd seen how shocked they'd been at the mere idea of leaving the Game Grid; he wondered what their reaction to his real identity would be.

Flynn dashed back up the ramp and listened as the sounds of the tanks filled the distance. But even as he listened, the sounds grew more distant.

He trotted back to the others. "They went right past us!" he told them, elated; light-cycles against tanks wasn't a sporting event he welcomed.

Tron responded, "We made it—this far." But it was farther, he thought, than he'd have expected. He and Ram and Flynn had done what had never been done before on the Game Grid. Perhaps this portended a change in circumstances, a chance to oppose the MCP. But Tron, scrutinizing Flynn, was still mystified by his daring and disregard of the common constraints.

A huge search force was deploying in the area. Tanks wheeled and raced, hurrying to assigned positions to run their patterns. Sark's Carrier presided over all; aboard it, the Command Program and his lieutenant studied the display of the situation on a broad expanse of wall-screen. Sark evaluated it, envisioning what the escapees were capable of doing, what they might choose as their best course of action, projecting himself into the minds of his prey.

He made a sudden decision. "Get the pursuit force back into the canyons." His eyes narrowed as he considered the screen. "Those programs never made it out of there."

While the lieutenant relayed his orders, Sark thought about the User and Tron, on the loose together out there. To him, they were a deadly disease abroad in the System.

"We'll have them in no time, sir," the lieutenant maintained with the confidence of one who holds no responsibility. "Long before they interrupt interface."

Sark glared at him icily for a moment, then turned away. "We'd better, null-unit." The lieutenant flinched at the affront, but dared say nothing. "I'll be lucky if the MCP doesn't blast me into a dead zone," finished the Command Program. "I want those conscripts!"

The lieutenant turned to a communications officer to summon more units, as many as it might take to saturate the area, and the vacant region that lay beyond.

Chapter Nine

RAM, TRON, AND Flynn hoisted themselves carefully up the cavern wall, finding fairly easy purchase on the geometrical protrusions. At last they reached an opening that they'd spotted from below. From there they surveyed the area. Their hiding place was located just inside the outermost wall of a vast megastructure, Flynn saw. The terrain fell away to a distant horizon; it was a poorly defined area of much lower resolution than the Game Grid and its immediate environs.

Beyond the rolling desolation of the electronic wasteland there was what looked like a cluster of large buildings, forms showing a meshwork of lights, a city reaching into the sky.

Flynn wondered if the MCP had any way of locating them in their current hideout, but decided that it was unlikely. The region was unpopulated, ignored by Master Control and its forces. He asked himself what had happened to the abandoned zone, how it had lapsed into a twilight region, and where its inhabitants had gone. The MCP and Sark answered the first question, of course. As for the second, Flynn assumed that the programs who'd lived there were now part of the MCP, some of them, and that others were Red Elite, and the rest consigned to the Game Grid—like poor Crom. And Flynn grimaced at the thought.

91

He looked to the others. "Well, do we pay a call on ol' Master Control?"

Ram stared at him in shock. "What—just the three of us?" When Flynn had led them from the Game Grid, Ram had been astonished at the innovation, deeming Flynn a daring tactician. But now, Ram wondered if Flynn wasn't well and truly glitched.

Flynn shrugged off the obvious hazards of the idea. "You know anybody's got an army for rent, that's fine. But my, uh, my User said to go take that sucker out." A twinge of honesty made him add, "If I don't get to the MCP, I'm never getting out of here." He thought of the massed troops of Sark and the MCP and wondered glumly if he had any real chance.

But Tron had caught his enthusiasm. "We can't get to the MCP without help from my User," he declared. "I have to get to that Input/Output Tower, communicate with him."

Flynn looked to where Tron was pointing. Near the center of the City was a tower, a resplendent cylinder lifting high in the air. *Input/Output,* Flynn seized on the words, *now we're talking! If only Alan and Lora are standing by . . .*

"Fine, check it out with Alan," said Flynn excitedly. "Maybe he knows what to—"

Something down in the chamber had caught his eye, a flicker of light. His fear that it was one of Sark's troopies or some odd and dangerous life form of the Electronic World was quickly quieted. It was a rippling blue phosphorescence, visible from that angle but not from where they'd stood on the cavern floor. It emerged from the ceiling of the place in glowing wavelets, an iridescent waterfall, to run down the wall and form a small stream, collecting in a pool there.

Ram, spotting it too, exclaimed, "That's just what I need right now!"

Flynn, puzzled, followed the other two as they scrambled back down and made for the stream. Ram flung himself down on the bank of the runoff, dipping his hands into it. To Flynn, the stuff he scooped up resembled a liquid; it was a fluid that emanated power. It give off light in soft blues and whites.

Tron and Ram both leaned down over it and drank deeply from flowing scintillation. Tron, pausing, pronounced with great enjoyment, "Ah, nice! You forget how good the power feels till you get to a pure source."

Of course, Flynn thought. The Master Control Program would certainly have governance over all the conventional power sources or outlets. Lower the programs' power and you keep them lethargic, dependent, obedient. But here in this ignored area, this trickle still ran unmonitored. Flynn pondered what it must feel like for Ram and Tron; no doubt the MCP kept User-Believers on pretty light rations.

"I feel much better," Ram announced, leaning back on his elbows, eyes squeezed shut with bliss. He seemed fresher, more vital and alive than he had been; the circuitry of his body shone more brightly.

"That's incredible," Flynn muttered. He lowered himself to lie prone, as they did, at the pool's edge. He scooped the stuff in his hands, his palms and fingers tingling with the feel of it. He sipped tentatively, then drank deeply. The liquid power had a wonderful taste he couldn't define. It spread a delirious warmth through him as it went down, livening and strengthening, lifting his spirits, renewing his sense of purpose. He could see that it was having the same effect on Tron, and on Ram, who now drank from his inverted disk as if from a saucer. Ram caught his eye and politely offered the disk; Flynn drank more.

Tron, stirring the rippling blue liquid with his hand, looked into it in deep concentration. Once, all programs had felt alive and responsive and energetic, as he was feeling; they could again. The sight of the City had made him think of Yori, as so many things did. His uncertainty as to whether or not she was still there was physical anguish. He channeled his yearning, putting himself into closer contact with the System.

"I can feel it," Tron said softly.

The tone of it caught Flynn. "Feel what? You okay?"

Tron felt a vague response from somewhere in the limitless awareness of the System. "Alan-One."

Flynn's heart—or whatever served a Warrior for one— soared to hear that. But he refrained from commenting, both to keep from distracting Tron and to avoid a complicated discussion. The Input/Output Tower it would be, then.

Tron pulled his hand from the eddied stream, rising to his feet in an easy movement that spoke of vigor and resolve. "Let's move out." He took up the handlebars that were all that had been left when his light-cycle had vanished; the others did the same. Tron gave silent thanks for the availability of power in the chamber.

The cavern's mouth was silent, dark, resembling any number of other such openings in the terrain. Unsurprising that the forces under Sark had passed by it in their haste to overtake the escapees—or so they'd intended—in the flatlands beyond.

A sound grew; the whine of engines echoed up from the throat of the cave. All at once the three light-cycles shot from it like torpedoes, once more in tight formation, their riders bent low over the handlebars.

Tron, in the lead, turned. Ram and Flynn kept close behind. They streaked through the desolate meanders of ledge and canyon, guided by Tron's instincts and memory, bound for the City. And Tron was bound, as well, for something as important to him as the end of the MCP's domination.

Is she still there? he asked himself, as he had countless times before. He put aside doubt; he would find her. He was free, with Ram and Flynn at his back.

Thought of Flynn brought back to Tron a brief report he'd heard of the combat with Crom, on the rings. He'd been heartened and surprised at Flynn's defiance in sparing Crom. Tron himself had been more than defiant in his time—Sark had lost plenty of game programs, guards, and Red Elite in *that* chase and capture!—but Flynn's disobedience of the Grid rules had won Tron's admiration. Still, he couldn't fathom where Flynn's amazing whims came from. They smacked of—Tron groped for the word—*autonomy.*

Tron returned his attention to driving; it was enough that Flynn was allied to him. Tron felt that the fact couldn't be without meaning, and somehow showed the hand of the Users at work. Flynn, meanwhile, leaned into the turns and kept pace with his friends, showing skill and a certain exuberance.

Not far away, a Game Tank turret swiveled, its gunner laying his cannon in on the three light-cycles. The machine maneuvered for a clear shot at the escapees, who hurtled out onto a long arch of bridgeway.

The gunner stared into his scope, his fire-control center rotating. A moment later, the fugitives entered his field of fire.

"Range: nine," chanted the gunner. "Mark: forty-five." He strained at his scope. "Forty-eight degrees. Hold it! Hold it . . ."

Tron flashed out across the bridge, Ram and Flynn spreading out to his rear due to the narrowness of the way. The gunner readied to fire. The cycles were suddenly within his cross hairs, their speed and direction pinpointed by his fire-control predictors.

"Fire!" the gunner barked. The glare of the main gun lit the tank. The gunner watched for its effect. The flaring, ruinous chevrons reached out, striking the span just where the cyclists rode. There was a blast at impact, brilliant force spewed in all directions, making it impossible for the gunner to see for a moment.

Flynn and Ram were thrown from their cycles. Oddly shaped fragments of the Electronic landscape landed all around them, concealing and partly covering Flynn and Ram. The round had struck the bridge just behind Tron. He skidded his cycle to a halt at the far end of the bridge, nearly losing control. Gazing back in horror, he saw that the bridge had been blown in half; a large portion of its central arch was completely gone. Of Ram, Flynn, and their machines, he could see nothing.

Face contorted in grief, Tron looked into the abyss. For Ram and Flynn to have survived the Game Grid, won their freedom, and come so close to the Input/Output Tower only to fall—Tron could make no sense of it. He let out a cry that was mourning, indictment, and plea, "NO-oo!"

He could see nothing in the chasm below, where modular rubble lay heaped. It didn't matter; there was no way that Ram and Flynn could have lived through such a fall. He could hear tanks maneuvering toward him, aware that one of the escapees was still alive. They fired as they came, angling, their salvos sending energy fountaining high into the air all around him. Tron thrust aside everything but his sense of mission, and revved his machine. He peeled down a narrow gully where tanks would be unable to follow, hoping that the ledges and landings would shield him from Sark's Carrier.

A practical side of his mind told him that if the search force was scouring the canyon area for him, the way to the City and the Input/Output Tower might lay clear. He began a roundabout course, to lose the tanks in the irregular terrain and get to the road to the Factory Domain.

Flynn held his head, wondering if somebody actually *had* beaten him with a crowbar, as he felt. He groaned, even though he found his skull still intact, and gave grudging thanks to the Game Grid for the durability of its helmets and armor.

He struggled to his knees, waves of dizziness and nausea assailing him. He heaved for breath, waiting for his vision to clear, and tried to put together what had happened. He'd been following Ram across the bridge . . .

The sound of approaching tanks broke through his pain, answering his groping questions. He spied a nearby form; Ram sprawled, unconscious or dead, unmoving. Flynn now recalled laying down the light-cycle as the blast had struck the bridge, and Ram had done the same. Both machines must now be at the bottom of the crevasse. *Just luck that we're not with 'em*, he realized.

Flynn labored to his feet, swaying a little, and stumbled over to Ram. The clamor of the armored detachment reminded him that he had little time to act, none at all to check on Ram's condition. He searched around him desperately for a hiding place and spotted a fissure in the rampart face a few yards away. Panting, pulses of darkness obscuring his vision every few moments, Flynn dragged Ram's body to the fissure and drew it in after him. There was barely room for them.

Just then a huge shape descended to hover overhead. On board his Carrier, summoned by the tank-force commander as soon as the escapees had been sighted, Sark peered into a viewscreen. Through high magnification he saw the remnants of the bridge span, the rubble and the heaped ruin in the crevasse below. He'd already had word that one cyclist had survived, and that units were tightening a search pattern around the area. Sark suspected that the survivor would prove to be Tron; he'd been the most capable of the three. That meant, at least, that Sark's worries with the User were over. But partial success wouldn't be enough to placate the MCP.

The column of tanks rolled past the spot where Flynn had taken refuge, looking for an alternate route across the gap in order to resume the chase. Flynn, already pressing himself and Ram as far back in the fissure as he could, tried to press back even farther. Tanks rolled by, smooth and swift, light-treads flashing.

He waited for them to notice him, to halt and train their guns on him or unbutton so that the crews could take him back into captivity. But the column moved at a rapid clip, never slowing.

The tankers' report went to Sark even as they raced after Tron: no remains had been found, and the other two cyclists were under a small mountain of shattered arch.

Bent low to his controls, Tron gave his cycle all the power it had. Here on the flat, open part of the domain, his only chance was speed. If searchers came after him now, there would be no concealment and little likelihood of evasion. The cycle was a yellow streak, the ground beneath it a featureless smear. He'd eluded the search pattern in the canyon area; he doubted he could do the same out here.

Above and behind him, Sark's Carrier was coming onto a new heading. Tron hadn't been found in the canyons, and if he wasn't located soon, the Command Program decided, that would mean that he'd somehow gotten through. He would then logically be on the way to the Input/Output Tower. Sark felt from the pattern that the survivor was Tron, without doubt. Sark was secretly, maliciously pleased; he wanted Tron to perish at a time and in a manner that he, Sark, could enjoy.

Flynn thought his vision was beginning to go, then realized that it was getting darker. Staggering under Ram's weight, striving to put one foot in front of the other as he seemed to have been doing for eternity, Flynn tried to tell himself that the darkness could only help him avoid recapture. That didn't keep him from feeling uncomfortable with the thought of being overtaken by night in such bleak terrain. Hiding, scuttling, ducking, with the unconscious Ram to carry and look out for, he'd somehow made it past the search cordons. The tankers probably assumed Ram and him dead. The search was geared to a fugitive traveling by light-cycle rather than one plodding through the narrowest passageways with another on his back.

He'd long since stopped taking in the view of a low-resolution, eerily empty landscape, except to try to figure out which way to go next. He'd stopped for frequent rests, and been boosted by the power he'd drunk. But even so, the endless slogging was wearing him down. Numbed by exertion, he tried to ignore the haunted feel of his surroundings.

He came down onto the flatlands, leaving the convoluted canyon-constructs behind. He reached the level region long after Tron had passed over it and Sark's Carrier had abandoned the hunt there. Flynn's plan was still to try to get to that Input/Output Tower. If Tron still lived—and Flynn couldn't shake the feeling that he did—the User Champion would be doing his best to get to it, too. If he couldn't locate Tron, Flynn planned to sneak into the Tower and take a cut at contacting Alan himself.

But for now he had Ram to think of. Abandoning the injured program never occurred to him; Flynn had fought alongside and shared deadly risk with Ram. He was incapable of seeing Ram as other than a friend and ally.

And so he trudged on, slowly covering the distance, drawing on some unexpected reservoir of strength. He wasn't sure how his new physiology worked, but, given the circumstances, he wasn't about to question its advantages. He passed into an area where piles of components and modules were scattered about or heaped like discarded toys. Polyhedrons, angular pieces, and segments of what once had been greater wholes were piled or strewn in every direction, their resolution low. Flynn decided to take shelter in the area, see what he could do for Ram, and give himself a chance to rest.

He came across a gigantic pit, hundreds of yards in diameter, filled with jumbled shapes and patterned oddments. Near the center of the pit, he saw, was a structure that reminded him of a blockhouse or pillbox. It appeared to have a doorway. Flynn resettled Ram's weight, braced himself for one last effort, and began picking his way carefully across the debris, stepping with extreme care, straining to see, trying not to think what would happen if some of the pieces should suddenly shift.

With a final lunge, using the edge of a fragment as a handhold, he drew himself up onto the object. It appeared sound, something like a bunker. That decided him; he would have concealment and shelter as well. He wasn't sure how weather in the System might manifest itself outside the Game Grid, so he wasn't taking chances. He entered cautiously, in case somebody or something else had already claimed the place as home or lair.

Inside, a faint glow suffused the air, a last residue of power. The entire front of the place was a single window. Short staircases connected several different sections or landings, all of them mounted with or giving access to instrumentation, control banks, or other gadgetry. A thing that might be a cannon or a telescope rode a low track that ran along the window. Flynn could make nothing of the pedestal, or whatever it was, fronting the window's center; it had an outspread cross-member and a central lever resembling an aircraft's control stick.

Perhaps later he could make some sense of it all, maybe even find something of use. He particularly wanted to know what he was headed into, what was going on in the System, and what had happened to Tron. But all that would have to wait until he'd rested.

He put Ram down carefully against the rear bulkhead of the place, setting him against an inclined surface at the base of it. Then Flynn collapsed to lie back, closing his eyes. But, oddly, that reservoir of energy began to restore him at once. He could feel it, a strengthening of some inner charge. Flynn's mind spun with the events of the past few hours. He tried to go completely limp, to relax; he couldn't recall the last time he'd stretched out like this. His hand fell, bumping a panel.

Energy jumped the gap between Flynn's hand and the panel, which then shone with renewed power.

Flynn's eyes shot open. Seeing what had happened, he stared in disbelief at his hand, which now glowed like a lantern. To find out if his senses were deceiving him, he leaned toward the bulkhead and held his palm up, slowly extending it.

An incandescent ray sprang from his palm to spatter against the bulkhead, which took on that incandescence. An instant later, the whole place began to shudder and quake. "What's going *on*?" Flynn yelped to himself.

He heard Ram's voice, thick with awe and some fear. "You shouldn't be able to do that."

Turning, he saw that Ram had been watching. "We're inside a Recognizer," Ram went on. "You can't steal a Recognizer."

Flynn laughed helplessly. "Are you kidding? I think *it's* stealing *us*." He gazed, stunned, at his sparkling hand. "Do you *see* this?" He turned it over, examining its bright circuitry. "Holy—"

He stood, holding his hands wide apart, concentrating, to find out what was really occurring. An arc of energy, dazzling and potent, leaped from his hand to one of the surfaces of the Reco's interior, imparting animating force. The long tongue of radiance sought various components, reactivating them.

Flynn didn't question what was happening; it was a phenomenon he could only partially control, and couldn't begin to analyze. His human origin, he concluded, gave him additional abilities in the System, abilities no program could match. The Reco interior was now bright with vivified systemry. Finally, Flynn felt it heave free of its interment and rise. He sprinted to the front observation pane, taking the low stairs in one bound.

He saw that he'd taken shelter in the Reco's head-module. It ascended, a hundred feet and more into the air, wobbling. As Flynn watched, another massive component rocked and shook itself loose from the clutter of the pit, lifting toward him; it was the sloping housing-collar in which the Reco's head had once been set. It gently settled in underneath the turret head and fixed itself in its former position, the binding field taking hold.

Other polyhedrons were levitating from the pit now, pieces of the central assembly that provided the main power source and operated the huge pincers. Lifting majestically after them came the pincers themselves, monolithic. Flynn, who'd conceived the Reco, watched through its eyes. Scattered parts reintegrated themselves and resumed unity. He didn't know which astounded him more, the event he was watching or the fact that he was responsible for it.

The Recognizer was holding place over the pit and the gaps in the heaped forms below, where its components had lain. Flynn waited for a few moments, but nothing more happened. It was as if something more were expected of him. He stepped over to the pedestal assembly at the middle of the observation pane, looking it over, studying its crossbar.

"This looks promising. Kinda like the old arcade grips." He took hold of the crossbar. Again, energy ran from him, to outline the instrument as Saint Elmo's fire had the masts of sailing ships. The Reco shuddered, then moved forward. "All right!" Flynn crowed, intoxicated with his success. "Smokin'!" He began to experiment with the controls. "Let's get this show on the road!"

Somewhat erratically, the Reco picked up speed. Flynn saw right away that controlling the huge machine was trickier than he'd thought. He took a quick glance back at Ram. "You okay? You don't look so good."

Then he saw that Ram's corona was darkening quickly, and knew the program's fight to survive was not going well. "We'll get you out of here," Flynn promised. "Hang on."

Ram's voice was slurred with pain and the diminishment of his aura. "How— how can you—" he said, then winced in pain, unable to finish.

"Never mind that now," Flynn threw over his shoulder, struggling to keep the Reco on course. "I gotta get us outta here, get you fixed up."

Ram painfully drew himself into a sitting position. When he strained to speak, Flynn could barely hear him. "Come here."

Flynn released the controls. The Reco halted, holding place. Flynn hurried to Ram's side and kneeled, not knowing what to say or how he might help. The first aid he knew was of no use here.

Ram clutched his hands; the grip was pitifully feeble. "Tell me who you are!" he begged.

Flynn gazed down at him, feeling futile, unsure of what to do. But he couldn't lie to Ram now. "I'm a User."

Ram's aura had flickered low, a dying nimbus. He stared at Flynn with the intensity of a man next to death. "Help . . . Tron," he implored. "Flynn, help Tron."

It was the last of his strength. "Ram!" Flynn cried, and as he watched, horrified, Ram's body began to break down, scan lines appearing as he faded from view. Flynn shouted his name again as Ram vanished, leaving Flynn's hands grasping at empty air. And then Kevin Flynn was alone, suddenly aware of how much the companionship of Tron and Ram had come to mean to him. To think of Ram as a program who'd de-rezzed was inconceivable; a friend and ally had died.

Chapter Ten

THE CITY HAD changed since Tron had last been there. Once a place as bright as the heart of a star, a place of activity and industry, center of the Factory Domain, it was now dimly lit except for the Input/Output Tower. Its once vigorous programs now appeared to be in a state of shock, or somnambulance. The MCP was obviously doling out its hoarded power very sparingly. The entire Domain was at a low state of resolution, much of it dark and two-dimensional-looking.

Tron steered for the Factory Complex, which lay near the City's center. There, he knew, some minimal level of activity would still exist. And there, too, he hoped to find the one who was most important to him.

When he'd neared the Factory Complex, he halted the light-cycle and permitted it to de-rezz. Discarding the useless handlebars, he took in his surroundings grimly, incensed at the cruelty and waste he saw. He trotted from the alleyway where he'd stopped, out onto a broad thoroughfare. Programs of all sorts walked there, many of them strangely shaped because of their functions.

There was a Warrior of a type not known to Tron. He had an energy lance cradled in the crook of his left arm; his right arm and part of his helmet had been blown away, leaving only long, trailing streamers of glowing filaments. A little light-exchange monitor, outmoded and enclosed in his glassy bulb, passed by. Tron had to step around a segmented connectoid that, crawling along like a huge, blind worm, nearly bumped into him. He recognized cryptarithmetic priests by their circuited cassocks. But there was little animation to anyone, and no enthusiasm. Tron saw one program speaking to another, and stopped to listen.

The program spoke in monotone as the two gazed at one another lifelessly. "Three hundred. Eight? Zero . . . forty-three."

Tron could listen no more. Shaking his head sadly, he walked along streets that had once been ablaze with productivity and drive. He spied his objective, the design and fabrication center of the Factory Complex. On the way, he stopped by two more programs to eavesdrop once more, unsure of how the recent changes might have affected local circumstances.

"Sixty-six," mumbled one of them stupidly. "Nine; seven-two-three-one. Mark four." Tron walked on. He approached the Factory Complex, a megacluster of industrial buildings and grouped production facilities. He was cautious, and that was fortunate. Stationed in front of the Complex's main entrance was a squad of Memory Guards, their staffs displayed conspicuously. Tron stepped back into the shadows— one small positive side of the darkening of the Factory Domain—and considered his situation, trying to recall the layout of the Complex. In the distance he could see the Input/Output Tower, and touching it just then was the bright Communication Beam that permitted programs to talk to their Users, reaching down from infinity. Urgent as his mission was, Tron had to find Yori first, for the help she could provide, in part, but in the main because—he had to find her.

Sark's Carrier cruised over the fretwork of byways, culs-de-sac, channels, and chutelike roads bordering the City. The craft was headed for the Factory Complex; Sark was certain now that he knew where his quarry would go.

Below, unnoticed by the Carrier, a Reco blundered and bumped along through the maze, bouncing off the high walls from time to time, now so low that it scraped the ground, now so high that its operator had trouble maintaining control.

Flynn stood before the eyeslit working the controls, tilting the crossbar and finger-stroking the touch-scales.

"Damn Reco!" he muttered, trying to maintain a delicate touch with the skittish controls. "Why can't it just go straight?"

He groused at himself for not having designed a better-handling, more stable villain for *Space Paranoids*. He was interrupted at it by something overhead, a sparkle from one of the pieces of equipment, right where a Reco's third eye would've been. Flynn looked up at it and it seemed to draw back warily. He turned away from it, nonchalant, pretending not to have noticed. The sparkle appeared again at the extreme corner of his peripheral vision.

The Bit edged forward, trying for a better look at Flynn. It came a little farther. Flynn whirled on it, holding up his hand with thumb and forefinger out as if it were a gun. "Okay; hold it right there!" He wondered what eerie new development the System was about to toss his way.

It was a glittering, faceted shape, nearly a sphere. The Bit cringed timidly, then saw Flynn's face. Thinking it had found Clu again, it came closer. The Bit expanded into a spiky green star and, overjoyed, shouted, "Yeah!"

Flynn checked the thing over suspiciously. "What d'you mean, 'yeah'?"

"Yesss," the Bit elaborated. It added, "Sure. Right!" Its spikes disappeared as soon as the Bit went silent, and it reverted to a faceted, shining sphere.

Flynn reminded himself that he couldn't just let the Reco stand dead in the air. He took hold of the crossbar once more. He asked the outlandish newcomer, "That all you can say?"

"Uh-uh," the Bit allowed. "No!" For these responses its spiny form shone red. Then it lapsed once more to its original appearance.

"Oh," Flynn mulled. "Anything else?"

"Absolutely," replied the Bit energetically. "Yup!" It had missed Clu terribly since taking refuge in the Reco he'd destroyed with his tank. It was deliriously happy to be back with him, but didn't understand why he had become so forgetful.

"Only yes and no," Flynn ruminated, brows knit. Then it dawned on him. "You're a *Bit!*"

"For sure!" the Bit confirmed, relieved.

"Where's your program?" Flynn asked, dividing his attention between the touchy Reco controls and the Bit. "Won't it miss you?"

"Negative," said the Bit with a note of confusion, implying that he'd asked a question to which he should know the answer. It flittered near him expectantly. He eyed it with a certain caution. It sure wasn't afraid of him, now that it had gotten a good look at him. The thought set something off. "*I'm* your program?"

The Bit beamed happily, a verdant sphere. "You betcha!" it told him in a congratulatory voice, with some relief.

Flynn sighed and went back to conning the Reco along. "Another mouth to feed."

In time, he became a little more practiced and a good deal more confident. He increased speed, and if the Reco's progress was unsteady and given to sudden veerings, at least he avoided slamming it into a wall. This was the sort of thing Flynn loved, learning a new skill, testing his coordination. For a while, he forgot his problems and played the Reco as if it were a game.

"Pretty good drivin', huh?" he asked the Bit smugly. Just then the Reco gave an ungainly lurch, coming close to one of the walls of the channellike route.

"No way," judged the Bit harshly.

"Who asked you?" Flynn snarled. He brought the Reco around the next turn in a wide, unsteady swing, its stabilizers complaining. "I'm getting the hang of it," he added. "Watch this!"

Lower lip between his teeth, he increased speed, making for the City. But he'd overaccelerated and was, after all, operating a machine that was usually run by a number of crewmen. The Reco tilted one way, then another, like a drunk. It slammed into a wall, bounced across and rebounded off the opposite one.

"Noo-ooooo!" the Bit wailed, flashing an emphatic red, sounding as if it would've enjoyed hiding behind something again.

"Hey, gimme a break!" Flynn protested. "They didn't teach Reco steering in Driver's Ed." But he refused to slow to a more sedate pace, deciding that here and now were the place and time to master the vehicle. *I'm getting this thing to the City if I have to dribble it there!* he vowed silently.

And so they went, the Reco caroming off the occasional wall and dividing its time between orderly progress and impromptu assaults on the sides of the channels. Flynn, driving with brio, cheered himself on enthusiastically. The Bit did not.

Inside the Factory Complex, workers along an observation window manipulated fabrication controls, intent on the most complicated simulation project the Complex had yet attempted. Taking shape before them in a vast hangar was the craft that Gibbs had seen pictured on Dillinger's desk, drawn from the concept of a Solar Sailer.

As the workers sat at their boards and screens, defining what the ship would be and how she would operate, the Solar Sailer herself came into higher and higher resolution, generated by the System. Voices murmured spiritlessly, "Transfer forty-nine," "Five-seven-eight-three," "Sixty-seven?" "Eighty-two," "Eighty-two," "Eighty-two."

One row of workers was made up entirely of female programs, one of whom was checking a diagram listlessly, mechanically. Once, she'd been a premier designer-coordinator, recognized throughout the Complex for her exacting and uncompromising work. But now she was reduced to the status of labor automaton. She wore a worker's aspect, her circuitry muted, complete with tight helmet-cap and boots.

From behind a nearby pillar, Tron watched her, appalled by her insensibility, afraid for her. The background of emotionless voices made the scene more bizarre and frightening. *Yori,* he thought, *even you?*

She rose and walked to one of the Memory Guards posted around the room. "Production input?" the guard demanded.

As if in a trance, she replied, "Three-zero-five-six. Ninety-nine. Limited four. Eight."

That appeared to satisfy the Memory Guard. As Yori walked away, he noted, "Twelve." What that might mean, Tron had no idea, and Yori did not react to it.

It hadn't taken him long to locate her; even in an enervated state, he had known, she would be virtually indispensable to the Factory Complex. Now, as he'd hoped when he'd selected his hiding place, she walked in his direction when she left the work area. As she passed by, Tron reached out to grab her arm and pull her into concealment with him. She yielded to it, oblivious, giving no sign of recognizing the one who meant everything to her, and to whom she meant the same.

"Yori!" he implored. She simply gazed at him.

"Nine," she recited. "Sixty-two. Four. Seven."

He shook her. "Yori!" She was unresponsive. In sudden decision he held his hand near her face, more thankful than ever that he'd come across free-flowing power in the cave.

Tron focused all his attention on Yori, and on the power he'd absorbed, carefully calculating the transfer he was about to make. Power beamed from his hand, not in a rush, but in a carefully controlled stream. It found the specific terminus, the circuitry-nexus at the base of her throat. They held their poses in that fashion for long moments as Tron poured new life into her. Yori's circuitry flared brighter.

Her expression changed, the dullness falling away. Astonishment took its place as she felt the transfusion coursing through her, as if she'd come back from de-resolution. Then she recognized him and broke into the smile he treasured. *"Tron!"*

She threw her arms around his neck and they embraced, laughing, holding one another close. He lifted her from the floor. "Yori! Hey—"

She hugged him again. She was nearly a head shorter than he, her figure at once slender and full. The high cheekbones and wide eyes were the image of Lora's. "Oh, Tron, I knew you'd escape! They've never *built* the circuit that could hold you!"

He looked around, remembering the guards. "We have to make plans. Where can we go?"

She saw the Complex around her with new eyes now that he'd restored to her her true personality, finding it difficult to remember the endless, mindless work there or the unthinking phantom who had been Yori for so long.

"This way," she said, taking Tron's hand. "Quickly!"

She led him by back corridors, toward an unguarded exit. Trying to keep to a conservative pace, they passed programs who moved with shuffling steps or stood stuporously, all but devoid of life. Some few showed signs of vitality, but not many. Tron listened in as they passed three programs huddled in conversation.

"Two-eight-two, unit four," one factory program droned as they passed. "X-sector to interface," a second replied, the third contributing, "With micronet zero-zero-zero."

Tron had paused. Now he asked Yori, "What are they saying?"

"Those are instructions for shutting down functions," she explained in a subdued tone. "If much more of this goes on, this System is going to collapse."

Tron regarded the muddled programs with pity and frustration. The Users had been so free with their power, he remembered; their only aim had been to solve problems, to achieve and create. The System had been filled with activity and accomplishment then. But the MCP wouldn't have permitted its subjects full power even if it had been able to do so and still feed itself to satiation. Master Control and Sark ruled, in part, by privation, keeping their subjects weak.

"I know, Yori," he answered her. "But things are going to change. I've got to get to Alan-One; he was going to tell me how to—"

He'd been opening the exit door they'd found. Yori's eyes widened as she saw something over his shoulder. She yanked him, skidding for balance, back inside; Tron had enough sense not to protest. They watched with the door open a crack as a Recognizer drifted up the street. Its mien was the perfect representation of the MCP's tyranny—never resting, never betraying emotion, always on the lookout, prepared to punish or destroy.

The Reco prowled past their hiding place as Yori suppressed an involuntary shiver. Tron held her more tightly. But the Reco didn't notice them, and continued its patrol. Yori led him off once more, keeping to the shadows. She might know a place of temporary refuge, he thought, but it was clear that there were no places of safety left.

In the City, some habitations were remnants of earlier times, not yet restructured or razed or consolidated. The MCP had been unwilling to divert resources for any such extraneous project, and so these places retained a scant minimum of livability. Leading Tron down a hallway in her building, Yori told him, "Dumont is in this City, too."

That was one thing in his favor, at least. Dumont the Guardian had always been friendly to him, and had a particular regard for Yori. One of Tron's main problems had been how to deal with the Guardian of the Input-Output Tower in order to gain access to Alan-One.

"Good." He smiled, squeezing her hand. "I˙can use his Tower to reach my User."

"I don't know," was her only reply, filling him with concern. Even Dumont, he knew, would have to pay lip service to Sark and the MCP. But if the Guardian were in fact in the MCP's service now rather than that of his sacred trust, it might spell ruin for Tron.

They came to a door that opened to the pressure of her palm on its scan-lock. The door disappeared, since the room beyond it would be occupied; personal privacy wasn't on the MCP's agenda. He followed her in.

It was an apartment of spacious rooms with a broad sweep of window that showed them the City from a height of many stories, but it was uncomfortably stark. There were two-dimensional remainders of furniture and decorations on the walls and floor, rigid, artless murals.

He frowned. "What's this place? It's terrible."

She took it all in with a wave. "My quarters. Not like home, is it?"

Not in the least, Tron thought. Not like that beautiful, crystalline place they had shared, with its spires of light and chambers of rich energy, filled with music and happiness and purpose.

"But we can talk here," she was saying. "Besides . . ."

Yori extended a palm toward a portion of the wall surface near the door frame. Into it she directed a precise measure of the power he had given her. The door rezzed up, returning to them a privacy Tron hadn't known since his capture. He realized now what an ache its absence had been.

And the flat images that had been part of the walls and floor were now shifting and changing, growing a third dimension, expanding like orchids opening in time-lapse photography. They took on color and texture, solidity and depth. The harsh illumination became softer, gentler, more subtle and pleasing to the eye.

Tron watched, bemused, but enjoying it all enormously. The floor and walls and ceiling altered; lounging surfaces and reclining areas burst forth, inviting relaxation, promising comfort. The entire apartment seemed alive. Decorative shapes and constructions, diverting and artistic, pleasant to behold, blossomed. Great care and thought had been given the decor; every last detail proclaimed Yori's hand.

Now Tron understood why she went through her work phases as did all the others, insensible. *How she must have to conserve her energy for even a brief period of this!* he thought. He touched a resilient seating-form; its warm, yielding surface was so different from the hardness of his cell—so different from what it had been only moments earlier. He watched the interplay of the scintilla-mosaic and admired the graceful geometries of a fan-shaped sculpture. He promised himself that the entire System would see such a renaissance.

Yori was watching him, taking pleasure in what she saw on his face. "That's—quite a trick," he chuckled. Then concern wiped his smile away. "But isn't someone likely to notice?"

She held his gaze. "I don't care."

They stood together for a time, then Yori broke their frieze, pointing to a hassocklike seating extrusion, urging him toward it. Tron sank down on it with the unconscious limberness with which he did all things. Yori seated herself on the floor before him.

"I can always count on you, can't I?" he said, not a question at all. Her absence had been the most painful deprivation inflicted upon him by captivity.

She leaned to him, laying a consoling hand on his knee, sorrowing for their long separation, celebrating him with her eyes. She confirmed what he'd said, made him understand all her feelings with a single word, "Always!"

With the entire System at his heels and no one else on whom he might rely, Tron felt at that moment the recipient of immeasurable good fortune. "How much time do we have in this room?"

Her lips curved, her look secret and yet open, plainspoken and at the same time oblique. Rising, sinuously graceful, she answered him, "Enough." She went to touch another surface in one of the walls.

An aurora appeared around her, gentle and triumphant. Yori transformed, brightened, as if shedding camouflage. Her helmet-cap was gone; her golden hair swirled and floated behind her. Tron watched, enchanted. She spent gladly of the power he'd given her. The worker's aspect fell away as Yori stood clothed in a cloud of splendor.

A diaphanous mantle fluttered around her, and the angular precision of her circuitry was replaced by lovely, delicate traceries, jewellike beads of radiance. She was like a magnificent, emergent butterfly, arms extended, the mantle rippling and billowing. She was completely herself again at last, the central thing in his existence, infinitely desirable. "Come here," she beckoned.

He stood and moved to her. The armor of combat sloughed away, and his helmet; they had no place here, and his circuitry took on a flowing look. His Warrior's forelock and queue were revealed, stirred by the forces around them.

Tron stood before her. "I love you."

They extended their hands until they nearly touched, palm to upraised palm. A blissful ray sprang between them, widening to envelop them, until they were like bright filaments. Celestials, they shared energy, were one. They sank down among the reclining-contours; the room shone with glory.

"I love you, Tron."

Chapter Eleven

FLYNN HAD NEVER played a better game.

The Reco—its guidance, the idiosyncrasies of its control system, the vagaries of its responses, the difficulties of maneuvering it through the relatively narrow avenues of the City, its tendency to yaw and drift—tested him as nothing ever had. He stood at the controls, straddle-legged, bending to the task and using body language just as he had in his own arcade. The Bit hovered nearby, observing without completely comprehending.

The Reco swung rather too quickly in response to Flynn's manipulations. It glanced off a building. "This honey doesn't handle so good in town," Flynn allowed by way of understatement, eyes snapping back and forth between the controls and the eyeslit.

"No!" the Bit seconded.

The buildings and other structures were closer together here. Flynn leaned over the crossbar, alert and eager, greeting the urban clutter as a sort of Advanced Reco Stunt Driving course. He saw the stuporous programs of the Factory Domain shake off their lethargy for a moment to gaze at the unusual behavior of his Recognizer. He hoped they enjoyed it.

He lost control and the machine side-slipped, clipping the

corner of a building, knocking loose large slabs of the building's side—the Reco was undamaged by such a minor collision. The rubble plunged to an empty street.

"I gotta stop this thing," Flynn advised himself through locked teeth.

"Yes-ss!" the Bit counseled.

But the Reco's controls didn't agree, and what Flynn had intended as a correction became an overcompensation. The giant machine banked toward the other side of the street, blundering into more buildings. Flynn, clinging to the crossbar, was whirled halfway around the control pedestal, legs wrapped around it. He began to regret that he hadn't experimented with the Reco's offensive weaponry. *How long'll it be before the cops show up?* he wondered.

A huge impact, the Reco jarring back against the opposite side of the street, threw Flynn away from the crossbar, landing him flat on his back. The Bit looped in close, worried about him. "I'm glad you agree," he replied with elaborate restraint.

The Reco hadn't stopped this time when he'd released the controls; he couldn't tell why. A bridge span loomed before it, a Game Tank stationed on the bridge's center. The Reco's pincers smashed completely through the span to either side of the vehicle; tank and bridge fragments dropped to the street.

This kinda romp's bound to upset the local gestapo, Flynn reasoned. He called it quits with the vehicle's controls. Struggling to his feet, he held his hands wide and reached into himself for the control and ordination he'd felt growing there. Power gushed from his palms.

"Right! Confirmed!" the Bit commented. "I couldn't have put it—"

But it was too late. The Reco had drifted too low; its pincers were knocked off by the first of a rising series of broad terraces. As the Reco hurtled on, a second terrace clipped its crosspiece and most of its midsection trusswork. The third caught the bottom of the housing-collar. That left only the Reco's head sailing forward, unpowered.

The head lofted in the general direction in which its erstwhile body had been proceeding. Flynn, bouncing within, gave a ululating yell, eyes bugging, watching the ground rush up at the eyeslit. The Bit circled and whizzed back and forth ineffectively, less concerned about impact than Flynn, but still very alarmed.

The Reco-head hit once, bouncing high. Arcing, it fell again. Its second bounce was less spectacular, but still gouged a deep hole in the street. The third bound was negligible by comparison. Moments later, it was rolling and bumping to a ponderous halt, still knocking free the odd chunk of building or paving. It came to rest against a glittering spire.

Flynn emerged, shaken but generally whole, staggering a little, dazed. Programs passed him without taking notice, so drained and numbed that they didn't even glance his way now that the Reco-head had come to a stop. He saw that they were far different from the programs of the Game Grid, only in part for their odd shapes and sizes. He almost forgot his landing, watching them go by like sleepwalkers.

"This town's full of live ones," he observed, wondering if they would even have had the presence of mind to dodge the Reco-head, had it come their way.

"Not a chance," the Bit contradicted, extruding its spikes and strobing red.

The furnishings and decorations in Yori's apartment had returned to their former two-dimensional state. The warmth of what had passed between them remained, though, despite what lay ahead.

Tron, seated cross-legged before the window, stared out at the shining Input/Output Tower, where the communication beam once more stretched from on high. He was torn between the desire to stay where he was and the knowledge that he must contact Alan-One. He followed the beam upward with his eye, wondering about its source, and the Users. He speculated, as he had so many times before, on what they were like, and what their World was like. So different that it was unimaginable, he concluded; so different that the mind of a mere program probably could not even comprehend it.

Soon his thoughts were back with Yori. He hated to take her into danger, but he might well need her help, particularly in swaying Dumont. And leaving her behind would offer her little safety; her life in the Factory Domain was slow death. He looked to the beam and willed with all his might that the immediate future would find him using it.

He heard her move to stand behind him, then kneel there. Yori's arms slipped around him. The embrace spoke her reluctance to end their interlude. Tron felt the same; their time together had strengthened him, revitalized him even more than had the deep draught of power in the cavern. She began, "It's—"

"—time to go," he said the words with her. He half-turned, sitting, watching her sad smile. Both had returned to their former appearance, arrayed as Warrior and worker. He rose, helping her up. They left the apartment. *For the last time,* it occurred to Yori, *either way.*

They attracted little attention in the streets. Even the occasional Memory Guard seemed to presume them to be of no more significance than any other program. They made their way toward the glittering Tower.

They encountered no guards at the doors of the Input/Output Tower; the place was virtually ignored now, forbidden. Tron supposed that the local programs lacked initiative to go there even if they hadn't been prohibited. He and Yori quickly found their way to a lift-platform, a large circular surface that gave access to the upper regions of the Tower. It raised, drawing level with a broad ledge-avenue. The two moved along it cautiously, amid blazing colors and the lights of Tower energy systems.

Without warning a Memory Guard stepped around a corner to face them with staff held in an attack grasp. Yori gasped; Tron responded as a Warrior was trained to—snatched his disk from its resting place on his back and hurled it before the guard could react. It struck the Memory Guard with a hissing explosion; he dropped his staff and collapsed to the floor, the glow of Tron's disk spreading over him.

Tron caught the returning disk and grabbed Yori's hand to pull her on. They leaped the de-rezzing guard and rushed on, unsure if the destruction of the guard or use of the disk had triggered any alarms. But they heard none, and saw no indication of pursuit.

They came to a hallway of cyclopean size, one that led to the Inner Chamber, where Dumont would be. At the corridor's other end was the door, a half-mile wide, which gave access to the Chamber, now three-quarters open. Near it was a cluster of Memory Guards. Peering from concealment, Tron looked around for some way to distract them or steal past.

Yori silently pointed across the vaulted corridor, and he
understood what she meant; while the stupendous door was
the main entrance to the Inner Chamber, there were others,
one in particular that was not so likely to be guarded. He
nodded to her plan, and they set off across the corridor. They
ran lightly, making no sound, but the corridor was so huge
that it would take long seconds for them to traverse it. As
they ran, Tron heard the sound he'd been dreading, a yell of
alarm from one of the distant guards.

Whether their movement had attracted the guard's attention
or a chance sideways glance had permitted him to spot them,
they never knew. Tron and Yori dashed to the opposite side
of the hallway as more Memory Guards took up the cry and
started toward them at a run. The two squeezed through a
narrow opening in the wall as Tron silently thanked the Users
that he and Yori were familiar with the layout of the Tower
as a result of their friendship with Dumont, perhaps more
familiar than the Memory Guards.

Tron slid a panel over the opening and secured it; a number
of such panels were in this area of the wall. The guards would
be delayed in finding the right one, then forcing it. The two
were in a utility shaft a hundred yards wide; it stretched upward through the Tower, crowded with coiled, intertwined
cables and lines and wires, some of them narrower than Yori's
little finger, some many times thicker than Tron was tall.

Selecting one of the widest cables, Tron started climbing,
followed by Yori. The two hauled themselves hand over hand,
finding abundant footing, ascending from coil to tangled coil.
The climb was demanding, and both were careful not to look
down. Yori watched Tron, using the purchases he found. Tron
listened constantly for Memory Guards' voices, for commands to halt. But none came; the pair struggled upward.

After what felt like hours of climbing and straining they
reached a ledge high above the corridor level. Tron dragged
himself onto it and helped Yori after. They paused, regaining
their strength and breath, leaning on one another. Again they
embraced, Yori running her hands over his chest.

Tron could bring himself to let her go only by an application of willpower. "Ready?" he asked, with a smile that was
an apology. She nodded; they started off along the ledge, past
the walls of service instrumentation and circuitry that serviced
the Tower. At the end of the ledge a window admitted a

strong golden light from the Inner Chamber. They stepped over twisted cables and thick bundles of bound lines, and peered down through the opening.

The Walls of the Inner Chamber, sloping inward toward their base at a 45-degree angle, were smooth and reflective, their incline even more gentle at the bottom. Far below was the main altar, raised above the floor on its circular dais, against one wall. Beyond it lay a darkened passageway. The main altar rested on a secondary one, this one fifty feet square. On the secondary altar was Dumont in his control pod; it was difficult to tell from where they watched, but he appeared to be asleep. The Inner Chamber was filled with a droning chant, a continuous reminder that this was the place in which the Users spoke. Being there again, Tron was unable to understand how any program could deny the existence of those who had created the System. Yori, too, was plainly moved at being within the Input/Output Tower once more.

A sound from the utility shaft interrupted them. They raced back to look down it, and saw a barge rising toward them, carrying guards who were inspecting openings and hiding places at every level, and examining the cables.

Kneeling on the shaft's rim, Tron watched the craft's ascent pattern. The very slow, methodical ascent meant that the guards had no idea where their quarry had gone.

"They don't see us," Yori breathed. Tron looked up at her. "I'll go first," she said, indicating the Inner Chamber.

"All right. I'll watch that thing." There might be danger ahead as well as behind, but the plan seemed best for now. Yori drew herself halfway through the window, then paused to give him a mischievous wink. Tron marveled at her courage. He held her arm as she lowered herself gingerly from the window, sliding onto the pitched surface of the wall. He took another look at Dumont, who hadn't moved, then released Yori's arm.

She began her long slide to the floor of the Chamber, gathering speed on the sloped wall, thankful that her durable working attire would protect her from friction. Tron, gripping the window ledge, watched her anxiously. Yori steered herself skillfully downward with hands and feet and by leaning her body. Tron returned to the shaft for a quick look, only to find the guards' barge rising toward him sharply. Somehow, they had spotted him. He heard the shouts of approaching Memory Guards.

Tron turned from the shaft at once and vaulted through the window with less regard for control than Yori had shown, gathering speed quickly. He doubted that the Memory Guards would follow him down the wall, since that would make them vulnerable to his attack at the bottom, and their craft would have to remain in the shaft. But a detachment of guards would be on their way to the Inner Chamber very soon; he had to deal with Dumont before they got through the titanic doorway.

Below, Yori slid to a halt out on the Chamber's floor, her momentum spent. She looked again to Dumont, whose eyes were closed, then up at Tron, who was swooping down the inclined plane of the wall faster than she had.

Tron skidded to a stop near where she sat and was at her side in an instant, gripping her shoulders. "Are you all right?"

Yori laughed and the big, alluring eyes shone. "That was fun! I should have used that entrance before!"

He looked back to the window. "The guards saw me. Come on!" He helped her to her feet and they ran toward the secondary altar and Dumont.

The Guardian of the Input/Output Tower was ensconced in his control pod; he and it were one. He resembled a sphinx rendered in instrumented, alien style, his circuitry aglow. The bulging headpiece which enclosed his face rose above him like a lofty miter, or the abdomen of some giant insect. He had no visible limbs or torso; he merged directly with the squat control pod.

As Tron and Yori reached the foot of the staircase leading to Dumont's altar, a hot defensive field began to radiate from it, forcing them to halt. Dumont's eyelids opened; Tron and Yori saw that he had been aware of their presence all along.

"Halt!" Dumont commanded, his voice aged and stern.

Confused and hurt by the rebuff, not understanding how a friend could act so, Yori exclaimed, "Dumont!"

The Guardian ignored that. "I can't stand all this commotion!" he complained in an irritated tone. Tron wondered if he meant only their own intrusion or the general furor they'd touched off. "What do you want?" Dumont finished testily.

Tron began tentatively, "I—I have come to communicate

with my User." It would have been such a perfunctory explanation at one time, and now it was a prohibited phrase.

"Hmm," Dumont considered it. Yori, hearing him, found herself suspecting that Dumont had already made up his mind, and not in their favor. "A difficult proposition; difficult proposition at best." His eyes swept the emptiness of the Inner Chamber. Their gazes followed his as he told them, "Not so long ago you could've come in here and seen programs lined up all the way back to those doors, waiting for communion with their Users."

He'd meant the doors at the far end of the gigantic corridor, but when he turned that way, Tron noticed that the huge innermost door was now closed, the Memory Guards shut out for the time being. That could only be Dumont's work. *But is it to protect us, or to prevent our escape?* he asked himself.

"But now," Dumont sighed, "this so-called Master Control Program is cutting programs off from their natural creators. Why, I could get myself de-rezzed just for letting you in here." He raised his eyes to the upper reaches of his province, observing, half to himself, "They *hate* this Tower. They'd close it down if they dared to. But they keep me around, in case one of *them* wants to deal with the Other World once in a while."

He sounded infinitely weary, disillusioned with a System where such things would be permitted. But his voice had held a particular distaste in speaking of *them*, the MCP and Sark and their servants. Perhaps there was a chance yet.

Tron took a step nearer, feeling the heat of the defensive field. "Dumont, my User has information that could—" He groped for the right words; mention of Sark and the MCP might have the wrong effect. "—could make this a free System again!"

Dumont's answer was a brief bark of scornful laughter. "Really," Tron maintained doggedly. "You'll have programs lined up around the block to use this place, and no MCP looking over your shoulder." He watched the old Guardian's face.

Dumont's voice held less sarcasm, more resignation. "When you've been in the System as long as I have, you hear many promises, many reassurances, many brave plans." There was, though, a note in his voice that spoke of a wavering, a suppressed desire to be convinced.

Yori walked up to the stairway, giving Dumont time to see what she intended, and the defensive field died away; he had always been fond of her. She came up the first few steps. "Dumont," she begged, and the name also held a certain sadness, a pity for the Guardian. A sound attracted her attention, and Yori glanced over her shoulder. "The guards are coming!"

Tron's eyes snapped back to the window through which they'd entered. Memory Guards were gathered there and, against his expectation, were preparing to descend the wall. He wondered how many armed, alert Memory Guards he could get with his disk if they reached the floor; those he saw seemed a high number.

He glanced back to Dumont, who was watching him, deliberating. "All right, all right," Dumont conceded at last, relief and peevishness mixed. The window abruptly snapped shut in the guards' cowled faces. Yori's expression held unutterable gladness.

"Who is your User, program?" Dumont intoned, in the formalized procedure they all knew so well.

Tron ascended the stairs halfway. "Alan-One," he proclaimed. "He calls me. May I pass?" There was more entreaty to the request than Tron had ever put into it before.

Dumont's voice was steady and dignified now, borne up by his faith. "All that is visible must grow and extend itself into the realm of the invisible."

The words appeared to fortify the Guardian, as Dumont was reminded of his own purpose and that of the System. Things had suddenly become clearer for him. Activating some unseen linkage within his pod, he rotated his altar a quarter turn; he swung to face the darkened opening that led to the primary altar.

Suddenly it was no longer dark, but a rectangle of light. It would permit access. "You may pass, my friend," Dumont announced quietly.

With a last look to Yori, Tron hurried up the steps. He paused for a glance to Dumont, lacking words to thank him. Then he hastened on, for the Communications Chamber.

Dumont sealed the opening after him and rotated his altar back so that he faced the staircase and Yori. She seated herself on a step with an affectionate look for Dumont. The Guardian was amazed to feel how at peace his decision had left him. Together, they waited.

Chapter Twelve

In the fortress of communication that was the Input/ Output Tower, all was confusion.

Squads of Memory Guards were trotting at the double, rushing to contingency posts or to reinforce those who were already at theirs, mustering as reserve elements or deploying to search. Conflicting orders were common; those in charge weren't quite sure yet what was happening. But it clearly centered on the Inner Chamber, and it was in that direction that most of the guardsmen went.

So it had been relatively easy for another intruder to make his way into the Tower.

Flynn peeked around a corner. "This is where Tron said he was goin'," he told himself. Finding the place had presented little problem, a simple casual stroll to the gleaming Tower, terminus of intermittent Communications Beams. But the Tower was enormous; where within it, Flynn asked himself, would the User Champion be? *Where all the action is,* he deduced glumly.

And he'd somehow lost the Bit. Whether it feared the Tower guards or was frightened by the Tower, he didn't know; he'd simply looked up to find it gone. Flynn missed it, though, and found himself hoping that the Bit was okay.

He made his way to a turn in the corridor and paused,

hearing the sound of marching feet. He looked around but could see no nook or other place of concealment. The smacking of boots against floor became louder. The Reds chanted "Hut! Hut! Hut!" in cadence.

Sark strode arrogantly, angrily, at the head of a double column of Red Elite and Memory Guards. He was confident that he would soon have his prey in hand, and meant to wreak terrible vengeance. The Command Program turned the corner to the next corridor and his troops followed. All of them stared directly ahead as they marched, with military precision. None of them thought to look up.

From the ledge where he lay flat, ten feet above the floor, Flynn looked down on the contingent. Recalling Sark's face in the mirror and Crom's falling to his destruction, Flynn hoped he'd get a crack at settling things with the Command Program.

But it was a good bet that Flynn wouldn't get very far in the Tower in the armor of a User-Believer. He noticed that the last of the Reds had fallen a little behind the others. He decided on a course of action and prepared himself. The files passed by beneath him, his objective still a little to the rear. Flynn bellied over the ledge and dropped down behind the program with no noticeable sound.

He'd come down a pace or so behind the Warrior. Flynn wrapped a fist, clapping his other hand to the Red's near shoulder at the same time. The fist swung as the Red did, a long, sloping right. Looking down on the decked Elite, Flynn didn't regret the throb in his knuckles.

A moment later, Flynn leaned over the inert program, working his fingers. He placed both hands on the Red's chest. The Red's aura pulsed, then began to siphon into Flynn, racing up his arms, changing his own aura to red as the fallen Elite began to de-rezz. Scan lines broke up the Warrior's structure. In moments, Flynn had absorbed the liberated energy, taking on the appearance of an Elite. Recalling their merciless extermination of the User-Believers on the Game Grid, he felt no sorrow for one of Sark's chosen Warriors.

Flynn glanced down the corridor to where the Command Program had disappeared. He padded after the troops, telling himself, "He's lookin' for Tron too." Sark or Dillinger, Flynn had a score with him.

He moved quickly and soon caught up with the column. Falling into place behind them, he looked every inch one of the Elite. Sark knew where Tron would go, and led his contingent without hesitation to the enormous door of the Inner Chamber. Tron's coming directly to the Input/Output Tower had been a move anticipated by Sark, but the Command Program had overlooked the possibility that Tron might use the utility shaft to gain access. And now the door remained stubbornly shut, keeping him from Tron.

Sark stared up wrathfully at the door. "The Tower Guardian is helping him, he *thinks!*" Sark hissed. He turned and commanded a lieutenant, "Bring the logic probe!"

Tron was at the summit of the Tower. When the Communication Beam was called down, its terminus was there, a bell-shaped housing with an opening at its top to admit the Beam. *The Communications Chamber,* thought Tron, staring around him, the urgency of his mission yielding for a moment to the awe he always felt in preparing to contact his User. Then he moved briskly, through the entrance at the base of the bell, galvanized.

Within the bell the floor sloped upward toward a truncated cone at its center. Tron climbed to the platform that was the cone's top, a circle scarcely wider than a pace. The platform had an inner luminosity, sign of the power residing there. Embedded in it was an intricate, layered assembly of circuitry. Tron glanced down at it, then up to the top of the bell. Beyond the opening, he could see only darkness. He settled his feet and collected his hands into fists held at his sides. His face underwent a change as he gazed upward, filling with anticipation and an excitement he couldn't suppress.

He slowly removed his disk from his back, taking it tightly in both hands, and raised it high above his head, staring upward, waiting. *The knowledge must come, and the instructions;* it was the function of every program to contact and serve its User. Tron wondered how Sark and the MCP could expect him to renounce this, even if refusal cost him his life.

There was a long anticipatory pause, nearly tangible. Then the beam flashed into being with an almost physical impact, shining down through the opening in the top of the bell. It illuminated the podium and Tron, proof of the Users' existence and attention. He held his disk high and felt the tug of the Communication Beam seeking to take it from his grasp. His hands began to shake with the exertion of retaining the disk, as the power of the Communication Beam built, an irresistible force. He felt exhilarated and humbled at the same time by this supreme power. The beam's strength increased; the disk was ripped from his fingers.

It rose slowly at first, then more quickly; straight toward the opening in the roof of the bell, riding the Beam. Tron stood, arms at his sides, watching it go, his figure nearly obscured by the wincing-bright glare.

Below, in the Inner Chamber, Yori and Dumont looked to one another, the power of the Beam illuminating the room around them. "It's begun," she whispered; Dumont only looked serene. They embraced hope.

Flynn watched the logic probe being brought down the corridor, an oblong, featureless package of disruptive power. It floated, suspended on an invisible supportive field of some type, passing the columns of troops, responding to the commands of some control mechanism or operator Flynn couldn't see. It stopped before the door to the Inner Chamber, and he noticed that even Sark was careful to keep well clear of it.

The logic probe fired multicolored lightning. The backwash of it lit the corridor, making Flynn and the others shrink back and shield their eyes. The door shook and, in moments, began to de-rezz. Sark watched the procedure with an ardent, poisonous smile.

Tron gazed upward, waiting, all his hopes pinned to the Communication Beam. All at once a voice filled the room, enormous, distorted, echoing like rolling thunder, familiar and yet alien.

TRON. TRON. LOCATION QUERY. LOCATION QUERY. CONFIRM.

He raised his voice to answer. "Confirmed, Alan-One," he called into the sky, to his unseen User, whose voice sounded so much like his own and yet so unlike it.

THERE YOU ARE! LOOK, BEFORE WE GET CUT OFF AGAIN, I'M GOING TO GIVE YOU SOME NEW CODING SO YOU CAN GAIN ACCESS TO THE MEMORY CORE OF THE MASTER CONTROL.

Tron knew a surge of exultation. At his User's instruction, images came into existence before him. A globe appeared, bound by grid lines that were wires of light, tiny sparks flashing at their intersections, a brighter sheen coming from its center.

WHEN YOU GET THERE, SEARCH ALL PASSWORD CODE SERIES——

The voice began to fade, obscured by static. "Wait!" Tron pleaded. "I can't hear!" But the voice of Alan-One was gone. His hopes dashed, Tron stood numbly in the wash of the Beam. *To have come so close*—he couldn't believe that such a thing had happened; defeat was a malignancy in him. He looked up once more, despondent. There was movement in the ray bathing him.

My disk! He reached up for it as it descended slowly; he took it reverently, jubilantly, snatching it to him, hardly able to believe his eyes. It was transplendent with a new light; delineated on its surface was the globe projected by Alan-One. He knew he held in his hands the key to a new order, and to an end to the MCP—if he could live long enough to use it.

Yori and Dumont watched as the great door de-rezzed before the irresistible onslaught of the logic probe.

"They'll be inside soon," she said, turning to Dumont, not knowing how she could apologize for the disaster. But she forgot that when she saw Tron standing in the doorway to the Communication Chamber. His stance was confident and erect; the purpose in him was plain. She knew at once that he hadn't failed; Yori said softly, "Oh, thank the Users!"

Dumont rotated his pod to follow her gaze, and saw Tron. "The time for delaying is over," the Guardian proclaimed. He was happy; he was as they had known him. Tron moved to his side with that strange, confident look, touching Dumont's pod, unable to show his affection in the time they had.

"Farewell, Tron!" Dumont bade. "The Users are waiting; the New Order is about to begin!" It was curious, Yori thought, to hear the Guardian so buoyant after all this time.

Tron couldn't delay long enough to tell the Guardian what had happened, and the certainty that Sark would interrogate Dumont made the telling too dangerous. So Tron said nothing and made only the gesture, to fortify Dumont against what was to come. Then he took Yori's hand, leading her down the stairs. Dumont watched, speculating on what it

had been that he had seen on Tron's face. When they got
to a small side door to the Inner Chamber, Dumont gave
the command that opened it just long enough for them to
slip through. Then Dumont was left alone, for the moment,
to watch the larger door de-rezz and contemplate Tron and
Yori, and to think of his own long life.

With a last burst of energy, the door dissipated in a swarm
of millions of dots of light. Sark stepped through the breach,
marching forward with files of Red Warriors and Memory
Guards at his back, his face a tightly controlled fury. The
Command Program was, the Guardian saw, at his most
ruthless and dangerous.

"Dumont!" he shouted as he drew near the altar. "Where's
that program?" Flynn, bringing up the rear, searched the
room for Tron but saw no one, and debated whether that
was a good sign or a bad one. Certainly, a fight, here, and
at these odds, would've been disastrous. With a shock, Flynn
recognized Gibbs' face on the being in the pod and wondered what the doctor would have thought if he'd seen his
doppelgänger.

"What program?" Dumont responded, pretending bewil-
dered innocence. "I'm sure you're mistaken."

Any additional time he could purchase for Yori and Tron
would be critical, Dumont knew; even the few seconds Sark
might devote to remonstrating with him. But Sark only glared
at the Guardian for a moment, fury undisguised. Seeing it,
Dumont trembled within his pod.

"Take him," Sark commanded in an even tone that was
more frightening than a bellow. The lieutenant and Memory
Guards moved forward.

They wended their way back to the Factory Complex, to
the design and fabrication center where Yori had worked,
attracting no notice from the apathetic programs they passed
in the streets. Their first need would be transportation to
get them to the MCP as quickly as possible, and Sark and
the MCP controlled all conventional means of travel. But
Yori had come up with a daring alternative.

And so they sprinted through Hangar 19. Above them,
suspended in her berthing field, completed, was the Solar
Sailer. She was an astoundingly beautiful vessel, speaking

of freedom and speed even though stationary. Her forebody was shaped like an artillery shell, with an aperture for the ejection of the Transmission Beam that drove her, situated in her prow. From the waist of the forebody radiated eight sparlike masts securing the great sails that fanned out to either side like immense metallic wings. Three long, thin antennae were set around her bow aperture to maintain beam connection and emission.

A single slender catwalk ran aft, the forebody's only connection to the midships. Midships was the bridge, a sort of rounded, bilevel quarterdeck. The Sailer's afterbody, a bulky, heavily shielded segment, served two functions, mounting the reception aperture through which the transmission beam entered the craft, and securing the vessel's rigging. Four long lines connected it to the deployed sails, its only connection to the rest of the ship. The Sailer suggested a dragonfly, delicate in appearance, perhaps 250 feet in length, afterbody included.

"This videogame ship—it's very fast," Yori told him. Tron considered the risks against the advantages. Riding transmission beams through the skies of the System would mean being sighted and pursued, and make them vulnerable to ground weapons as well, but they could take a roundabout course to minimize those dangers, and the craft's speed would help. More, she was the quickest means of getting to the MCP. That decided him.

They went to the lift-platform. It levitated them into the air, carrying them upward and passing into the center of the midships bridge, becoming part of the vessel's deck as it came to rest. They ran to the control console of the rounded bridge, and Yori bent over it worriedly, calling to mind all that she knew from her work in the Factory Domain, and finding it odd to draw on those torpid labor shifts.

Checking a map of the System, she examined the various transmission beams that crisscrossed its skies, the transfer points and origin fixes.

"It can take us across the Game Sea," she concluded, "out of this Domain, back to the Central Computer." Tron judged that that would be all he would need. Once in the Central Computer, he could follow Alan-One's instructions and use his disk.

The reverberations of footsteps on the catwalk brought him around in alarm. A guard was charging at them.

Tron pulled Yori back out of the way just as the guard leaped up the free-standing steps to the bridge. He kicked the guard squarely in the middle; the program fell back just as a dozen more swarmed up onto the Sailer.

Tron moved forward a little to confront them, waiting, disk held ready, knowing that every cast had to count. He crouched, threw. The weapon sliced air and smashed into the massed guards, halting their advance and downing two of their number, whose auras gave way to that of the disk. Then the whirling plate of light was back in his hand again. Tron saw, from the corner of his eye, more guards running across the hangar floor toward the Sailer.

He cast again and again as the guards bore down on him, driven by their fear of Sark and the MCP to face his defense. Many of them fell; more than enough were left. Knowing that he must keep them from Yori, so that she could pilot them to safety, he threw himself headlong at the advancing guards, striking out at them with hands and feet, throwing them overboard, driving some back against the others, hoping that no reinforcements would come over the rail behind him.

Tron called into play all the battle skills, strength, and speed he'd developed as a Warrior, and the power given him by Alan-One, battling as if possessed. Sark had come just short of killing him on the Game Grid but, in so doing, had honed him into the perfect fighting machine.

A guard sprang to swing a staff at him. Behind the guard, an Elite was crowding close, though he didn't seem to be ready for attack. Tron caught the Memory Guard's staff at its insulated points and yanked with all his might. The guard flipped backward and sideways, taking the disorganized Elite with him, as Tron had intended.

And then, incredibly, the catwalk was clear. He looked around; Yori was patting and stroking calmly at the ship's controls, safe. Searching for any other antagonists, Tron spotted a final guard standing atop the Sailer's forebody. They stared at one another, the guard plainly distressed by what he'd seen but knowing what it would mean to fail Sark.

Tron took a step toward him, and another, like some great, stalking cat. The guard gulped, looked down over the side, then glanced back to Tron. Deciding that he had a better chance of breaking or surviving a fall than he had against the User Champion, the guard jumped from the Sailer's forebody, aiming for a resolution emitter.

The Sailer lurched. Tron was thrown backward to fall sprawling. He looked aft to where Yori's finger traced the circuit paths on the controls, energy flowing from her fingertip. "We're off!" she called triumphantly.

A transmission beam passed into the receiver aperture in the ship's stern to reappear as a projection from her bow, emerging from the nozzle there like some mighty searchlight, driving the Sailer on her way. Her sails curved, full and taut to either side. The craft moved, lifting slowly at first, Yori easing them out of the gargantuan hangar, then accelerating sharply once in the clear, and gaining altitude. In seconds, she'd left the Factory Complex behind. Tron spied Sark's Carrier off in the distance, but knew that the Sailer was out of range of the warship's weapons, and that even the Carrier had no hope of overtaking her.

On the Carrier, Sark, immobilized in his podium, saw hanging before him the projected image of the MCP. The Command Program writhed in agony as the MCP applied pain to him through the power outlets in the podium. Its voice was chilling, implacable, and hateful, yet honeyed. "I hope you've enjoyed being a Command Program, Sark," it told him with slow menace. "I wonder how you'll like working in a pocket calculator."

Gasping, battered back and forth in torment, Sark managed, "We did take care of that User you sent us—"

"Yes! And now you've got two renegade programs running all over the System in a stolen simulation."

Another wave of pain rose through him as Sark was shaken again. "We'll get them!" he promised, barely able to breathe. "It's only a matter of time!" He wouldn't permit himself to think of what would happen if he didn't recapture the two; this was only a taste of the punishment the MCP was capable of meting out. He, who was the favorite, Champion of the MCP, was also in danger of being its most pitiable victim.

"I don't *have* time, Sark," the venomous voice told him. "And neither do you. End of line."

Nevertheless, the Carrier swung onto a pursuit course, after the Sailer. And even in his anguish, Sark knew a twinge of victory; this was a tacit admission that, after all, if he couldn't apprehend the fugitives, no one could. The Carrier shone with brighter resolution, its power increased by the MCP.

Chapter Thirteen

||||||||||||||||||||||||||||||||||||||||||||||||||||||||||||||||||||||||||||||||||||||||||||||||||||||||||||

OVERCOMING HIS SURPRISE at the Solar Sailer's acceleration, Tron hauled himself to his feet. He started back to where Yori manipulated the vessel's controls on the bridge, treading the catwalk lightly, watching the landscape slide by below at tremendous speed. Then something caught his eye and he paused, poising for battle, ready to bring forth his disk.

Yori, seeing it, called, "Tron, are you all right?"

He waved to indicate that he was, but said nothing, moving to the rail. Red fingers gripped it, in a precarious hold. One of Sark's Elite had somehow managed to cling to the rail. Tron peered over it and saw him dangling there, legs thrashing in a futile attempt to secure a foothold and draw himself onto the catwalk.

Tron had his disk out now. Without compunction, he raised it, intending to bring it down on the hands and send the Red back to nothingness.

The Red looked up in panic; Tron recognized him just as he yelped, "It's me! *Flynn!*"

His eyes were wide, riveted to the disk which threatened to smash his hands from the rail. "Flynn!" Tron yelled, amazed, replacing the disk on his back.

Flynn gave an embarrassed grin. "Greetings, program!" he panted.

133

"You're alive," Tron said, turning that concept over in his mind and seeing that no fact was absolute.

"Yeah, I—oooops!" He'd begun to lug himself up again, but his grasp had slipped. Tron's hands were at his wrists instantly, hauling him up while Flynn's boots scrabbled against the Sailer's hull for purchase. Tron's strength surprised him, even for a Champion; Flynn found himself drawn up over the rail with relative ease. He collapsed against the bulwark, breathing rapidly, watching the electronic landscape go by. It had been a close scrape; he had several ideas about how software-engineering-degree programs should be broadened, for survival's sake.

Sark's intuition about Tron's whereabouts had been correct. From what Flynn had been able to gather, the Command Program had quickly surmised that Tron and whoever was with him would seek the very fastest means of getting out of the City, and that had meant the Solar Sailer. By shuffling forward at the right moment, head lowered, Flynn had gotten himself selected as one of the Reds assigned to race to the Factory Complex to reinforce the guards there. The balance of his detachment had returned to the Carrier, apparently at the express order of the MCP. He and the Reds among whom he'd been hiding—many of them unknown to one another, allowing him to go unnoticed—had arrived just as Tron had been hijacking the Sailer. Racing along the catwalk to conk a Memory Guard, he'd been the victim of Tron's ferocity.

As Flynn leaned against the bulwark, he had time to reassert control over the energies and fields that constituted his body in the Electronic World. He focused his concentration; the Red glow faded; he returned to his former appearance. Tron watched in fascination, speculating once more on just who Flynn was and where he'd come from.

"Who is this?" asked a voice Flynn recognized. He turned and saw Yori, the eyes and the lips and the prepossessing lines of her face. He silently mouthed, Lora! But he saw his mistake in an instant, and kept himself from naming her. But he took a step toward her and Tron, not sure why he did, interposed himself with an uncertain smile.

"Flynn," Tron explained to the shimmering woman, as Flynn saw that they were a bonded pair and thought again what a strange mirror the System was. "Where's Ram?" Tron finished, turning back to him.

Memory came in a flood, saddening the reunion. "I'm sorry, Tron. He's—he didn't make it."

Tron lowered his head sadly, remembering the last concussion of the tank's cannonfire, the havoc of it. He'd written off both Flynn and Ram; odd now, to feel Ram's death all over again, with even more intensity. Flynn was thinking that he had at least found Tron, as Ram had urged him with his final breath.

Tron set aside grief, turning to Yori. "This is Flynn, the one who set me free." That wasn't quite the way things happened, but Flynn accepted the compliment with a grin, as she gave him an appraising look; Yori's reserved gratitude was worth more than effusive thanks from some other. She was a revelation to him: her essence was that of Lora, transfigured into a radiant creature, still very much like the woman he remembered.

"Then, I owe you some thanks," she said after a moment. Flynn dismissed it with a rather dashing shrug. "No big deal. I *ought* to know my way around that light-cycles routine. I mean, I *did* write the program for it." *Even if Dillinger got the stock options and the promo!* he amended to himself. That brought him back to problems at hand.

Now Tron was looking at him, troubled. *Flynn has a way of using the most peculiar phrases,* it occurred to him. Yet, he could see that Flynn had made no slip, and that there was more to it than that. "Wrote the? . . ."

"It's time I leveled with you, Tron," Flynn admitted, hoping they'd be able to accept it. "I'm a—well, I'm what you guys call a User."

No trumpets or drums, no light from on high; just an ordinary-looking program in conscript's armor. They gaped at him. A small part of Yori reasoned that part of the awe surrounding the Users was that they'd always been unseen; they had, for her, always conjured up mental images of huge, imperious beings, powerful and wise beyond belief, pursuing incomprehensible ends, shaping the System. Flynn did not quite measure up to that.

But he was, undeniably, not just another program; she'd heard of him from Tron, and seen him shed his Red aura.

She could not hold back all of her awe. "A User? In *our* World?"

Flynn nodded sheepishly. "Guess I took a wrong turn somewhere."

Tron labored with this revelation. It implied so much about the System, about purpose and function and the Users that he couldn't deal with all the doubts and questions that poured into his mind. And then again, regarding a former cellmate as a deity would take some getting used to. "But," he said slowly, "if you're a User, then everything you've done has been part of a plan?"

Flynn chortled, unaware of how much it shocked and alarmed Tron. "You wish! Man, I haven't had a second to think since I got down here. I mean, *in* here." He suddenly looked baffled. *"Out* here. Whatever."

Tron struggled to deal with that. Yori scrutinized Flynn curiously, accepting his claim for the time being, reserving final judgment. "Then . . ." Tron began, but let it trail off.

Flynn, exasperated and feeling a little guilty without understanding why he did, saw that he'd better make matters as plain as he could, to avoid confusion and keep them from assuming he was something he wasn't. He didn't want them relying on his nonexistent divinity if it came time to show hands. "Look, you guys know how it is. You just keep doin' what it looks like you're supposed to, even if it seems crazy, and you hope to Hell your User knows what's going on." There was curious satisfaction in having encapsulated the only truth he'd learned in either World.

Tron was still dubious. "Well, that's how it is for programs, yes, but—"

"I hate to disappoint you, pal," Flynn interrupted him, "but most of the time, that's how it is for Users, too."

"Stranger and stranger," Tron mused, wondering where the hierarchies ended. Yori was speculating on how Flynn's continued presence promised to change the System utterly, MCP or no MCP.

"So," Flynn resumed, patting Tron on the back, taking in the Solar Sailer, "nice ship you got here. What's our next move?"

Under the circumstances, Tron was not unsurprised to find that he was still in charge. "Remember, you wanted to pay a call on the MCP?" And Flynn's expression confirmed.

"We're on our way." Tron held up the altered disk. "Alan-One gave me the coding we need to go up against Master Control."

Good goin', Bradley! thought Flynn, and laughed. "Awright! Thank God Alan stayed awake, at least!" Again they were at a loss. The casual use of Alan-One's name, the easy familiarity of it, scandalized Tron.

Meantime, Yori considered what Flynn had just said, asking herself, thank *who?*

Sark's Carrier cruised the System's skies, hunting. The Command Program stood alone in thought, gazing out the broad pane of the bridge's observation window. He knew that the key to the Solar Sailer lay in her need to use the network of transmission beams that divided those skies, but the beams constituted a tremendously complicated webwork covering much of the System. And Tron hadn't been foolish enough to head directly for the Central Computer Area; the User Champion might be coming by any of a great number of possible routes. The Carrier must bear the major part of the responsibility for search and apprehension; Recos were too slow and short-range to be of much use. But: that Tron would come, Sark was positive.

And there was another possibility for intercepting the fugitives soon; Master Control was giving the transmission-beam network its attention, attempting to get a fix on the Sailer and interfere with her operation if possible. Sark repressed his impatience, his desire to come to a reckoning with Tron. He berated himself for not having had the User Champion brought before him on the Game Grid long ago, and slain him. But he'd always found Tron to be a curiosity, and so had increased the odds gradually, to find out precisely where the breaking point would come.

Except that instead of breaking down, Tron had broken out.

Sark's lieutenant spoke from behind him, quiet and diffident. "Sir, what do you want done with the Tower Guardian, Dumont? Put him in with the others?"

"No, bit-brain," the Command Program growled. He whirled on his subordinate with a brittle smile. "Prepare him for inquisition. I need a little relaxation." The idea soothed him; punishing Dumont would be a pleasant diversion until he had Tron in hand. "But first, rez up the Carrier for pursuit."

He considered his humbled lieutenant. The program might be loyal, but then again, it wouldn't do to have his servants taking the initiative. Sark's own status with the Master Control Program was too fragile right then to allow for possible rivals. "And one more thing," he finished balefully. "Don't think anymore. *I* do the thinking around here."

The fear and foreboding in the lieutenant's face reassured him. Quailed, the officer scurried off to do the Command Program's bidding. Sark returned to his contemplations in a more positive frame of mind.

Flynn studied the Sailer with great interest, reveling in her. He recognized her, now that he'd had the leisure to, as a simulation for a videogame, one drawn from NASA concepts but operating, here in the System, on different principles from a true Solar Sailer's. At any rate, Flynn was inclined to wager that it wasn't photons pushing her along.

The transmission beam entered the wide muzzle of the receiver in the afterbody far astern, to emerge from the ship's bow projector. In between, as far as Flynn could make out, it filled the gleaming metallic sails and drove the vessel at amazing speed, all in some invisible manner. The details of her construction were as fascinating as the Solar Sailer's motive power. What, for example, was he to make of the free-floating steps between catwalk and bridge, which stayed conscientiously in place, hanging in the air, without benefit of support or bracing? *Only that they're not the weirdest things I've seen,* he concluded, which he couldn't have said until recently.

He turned to Tron, who sat next to Yori as she piloted, his arm around her shoulders. He still looked strangely at Flynn, uncertain what to think or say about some of the things he'd heard, or even what questions to ask. "What about our friend Sark?" Flynn asked.

Tron ruminated on that. "Probably decided not to pursue us," he concluded. The Carrier could never overtake the Sailer; Sark's probable move, if he was still extant, would be to mount guard over the Central Computer Area. And Sark had failed the Master Control Program, not once but several times; it might have lost patience with him. "Programs have a way of just . . . disappearing, here."

"Not us, I hope," Flynn offered, seriocomedic.

Tron shook his head and held up his disk. "Not with this." It was shining in his hand as if impatient to perform its office. Tron looked to his mate and pilot. "I'm going to check on the beam connection, Yori. You two can keep a watch out for grid bugs."

Tron paced forward along the slender catwalk that still seemed awfully insubstantial to Flynn, though he knew it to be amazingly sturdy. He gazed after Tron, asking himself what in the world a grid bug was, and hoping that the beam connection—to which he'd given no thought whatsoever until this moment—was healthy and sound. He sure didn't want to see the Solar Sailer jump her rails, or whatever the term might be.

He looked to Yori. "You know the territory?"

She nodded. "A little."

Flynn, scanning the terrain below, pointed to a region that was unlit, apparently blighted, its features all two-dimensional and meaningless. He pointed to it. "What's wrong with that area?"

She rose up a little in the pilot's seat, saw, and replied with sadness: "The MCP blasted it. There are very few Domains left with any power at all."

He searched in all directions over the Game Sea, the expanse of liquid coming beneath the Sailer. With the exception of the blasted area, the Sea now stretched in all directions, phosphorescent, before them. It was lustrous, with breaking swells of multiple colors, horsetails of light, spray that resembled myriad stars. A strange, beautiful, mysterious place; he recalled the flatlands, the Factory Domain, the System as he'd seen it from high overhead on his descent, the stupendous megastructure of the Training Complex. The Electronic World was grotesque and menacing at times, but he couldn't deny that it was beautiful, enthralling at others.

No man had ever seen a more bizarre place, or had a more fantastic adventure. But if all went well, if the light was green at the Central Computer Area and Tron's disk worked out, Flynn supposed he'd be redigitized right away. With a million questions unanswered and the bulk of this cosmos unvisited, he would go home. It surprised him how much he regretted that part of it.

"They say there are creatures out on this sea," Yori was telling him. "Huge grid-eaters, and data pirates."

"Terrific," Flynn opined wryly; maybe going directly home wasn't such a bad idea after all. "Can't *wait* to meet them."

Yori had returned to her piloting. "Well, in any case, this beam can outpace anything on the Sea, including Sark's Carrier."

Thinking about interception courses rather than an aerial drag race, Flynn refrained from comment. The Game Sea, opalescent currents pulling colors this way and that through it, slid by underneath.

Tron stood on the very edge of the Sailer's forebody, straddling the bow and the beam-emission device itself, the vomiting of power. He held his disk before him, looking down at it, summoning to mind the words of Alan-One, trying to fathom the secrets of its modifications.

The transmission beam issued from the Solar Sailer, beyond the limits of Tron's vision. At varying distances and angles, other beams intersected it or ran by it in skew fashion, an exotic web of power and speed. Satisfied that the vessel's beam connection was secure, he drew back, putting all his concentration into the cast. He released, and the disk skimmed out from the ship, up and up, until it was nearly lost to sight.

The disk spun and flew, strobing its power, guided by his throw and will, rising. Tron followed the cast, studied it, evaluated every aspect of it. He hoped that it would serve the purpose for which Alan-One had refurbished it, and that his throw, when the time came, would be fast and accurate. All that Flynn had said, all this talk of Users, Tron knew, he must set aside. He could afford to harbor no doubts, no ambivalence, when time came to use the disk. There must be only Warrior, weapon, and target.

His disk had slowed now; it returned smoothly, as he'd intended. He watched it, squinting, evaluating. The disk picked up speed on its descent, as if keen to return to him. Tron reached out; it slammed into his hand with reassuring impact and a starburst of energy. He held it so for a moment, inspecting it once more, deciding at last that he'd found no fault in it or in his control. Tron was content; Flynn's being or not being a User was unimportant in this regard. No doubt or revelation had impaired his ability to use the weapon given him by Alan-One.

The Carrier scouted over the Game Sea as it moved toward the Central Computer Area; Sark's evaluation of the strategic situation was little different from Tron's. Still, his crew attended their instruments closely and kept vigilant watch from posts on the bridge and elsewhere aboard.

In the craft's interior, in a compartment reserved for Sark's most dire work, Dumont was experiencing sensations he hadn't known in a very long time: shock, fear, and, worst of all, pain. He was no longer the part-program, part-mechanism he had been in the Input/Output Tower. Bereft of his special status, his power drained, he'd reverted to a more conventional-looking sort of program, elderly, arrayed in flowing robes. But he was haggard, and spent from learning the torment of Sark's inquisition.

Memory Guards' staffs against his chest, he was imprisoned in two foot sockets that sizzled with punishing blasts, bringing pain that threatened his hold on sanity. But Dumont, face grooved and contorted with determination, denied them any added satisfaction, any show of surrender. It demanded every shred of willpower he could muster to keep from screaming, from begging them to stop, even though that would have done him no good. The ancient, seamed face was hardened with resolve. Another surge of excruciating power climbed from the boot sockets, bringing tortured convulsions; the guards kept him pinned to the wall with their staffs. And still there was no outcry from Dumont; that one thing, he'd sworn to deny them.

He was in a cell in the Carrier's capacious brig. Above him, the old program knew, Sark gazed down with vast enjoyment, delighting in the spectacle of suffering. Dumont's eyes, screwed tightly shut during the ordeal of the energy blasts, opened slowly, with great effort. He glanced up at the Command Program, knowing how Sark savored the scene. Cast down from his Guardianship, reduced to helplessness,

Dumont vowed that Sark would not have the satisfaction of seeing him break.

"Had enough?" asked the looming, helmeted figure above. The question had little meaning; there was only one way in which this process would end. Dumont lifted his pain-racked, infinitely tired eyes, nearly at the end of his resources.

He croaked upward, "What do you want? I'm busy."

Anger flared from the hateful face; Dumont knew a fleeting, intense triumph. Sark's win wasn't complete so long as the old program refused to give in. The rage that crept into the response indicated that. "Busy *dying,* you worn-out excuse for a program!" The air seemed charged with Sark's anger. Dumont took meager comfort from that.

"Yes, I'm old," Dumont admitted, as much to himself as to Sark. Grown old in the service of the Users, grown weary in the ceaseless functioning of the System, grown disillusioned with the wrongs he'd seen. He'd thought he had acquired the necessary defenses to coexist with the MCP and Sark. But somehow Tron and Yori's idealism, their hope, had stripped those away. The Guardian was surprised at how lightly this ultimate disaster, the storm of Sark's vengeance, weighed on his sense of self-preservation. Dumont knew he would soon be de-rezzed, but felt that he had rescued a certain part of himself.

Now he looked up again. "Old enough to remember the MCP when he was just a chess program," he added. His voice gathered certainty, though its volume rose only a little; Sark listened despite himself. "He started small and he'll end up small," finished Dumont.

Though Sark recovered almost instantly, there had been that moment's doubt on his face that made it all worthwhile for Dumont. "That's very funny, Dumont. Maybe I should keep you around, just to make me laugh."

And with that, another piercing blast came from the foot sockets. Dumont threw his head back in anguish and, in the all-embracing torment, lost the contentment he'd drawn from goading Sark, regretted it, disavowed it, and wished only for the suffering to end. But when it ended, Dumont, fully aware that his inquisition had only begun, drew peace from the knowledge that he'd thrown his tormentor off stride, if only momentarily, with the truth.

Then the sockets hummed again; the agony returned. Dumont was disfigured with it, misshapen, weeping. He wished only for the nothingness of de-rezzing. But one side of him marked how peculiar it was to feel a sense of satisfaction at having helped Tron and Yori in their hopeless mission, a sense of pride in having done his best in a World gone mad.

Chapter Fourteen

THE HORIZON HAD broken; Flynn knew that expectation that comes near the end of a long journey.

"We'll reach the end of the Game Sea soon," Yori announced, still at the helm. Her endurance there, her calm control and expertise, had not surprised him so much as reminded him of Lora. Yori exhibited that same commitment to see a thing through, to do what she was doing as well as it could be done, and leave no room for criticism. She had that same drive to settle for nothing less than excellence, and to settle for that only when perfection wasn't possible. Flynn, watching her, recalled all that Lora had meant to him.

Then he turned and watched Tron, who strode aft down the catwalk. Flynn thought about his disk cast from the bow, the precision and exuberance of it. Despite all he'd learned, Flynn knew that Tron had an affinity for the disk which he, Flynn, could only guess at. *Am I seeing Alan Bradley?* Flynn asked himself, looking at the gleaming User Champion, otherworldly Warrior in electronic armor. *I underestimated him. And Dillinger too, but in a different way, and Gibbs. And Lora; most of all, Lora.*

Flynn looked to the horizon once more; they were nearing the Central Computer Area, the MCP, and some final resolution—victory or death. Flynn decided that he wouldn't have had it any other way. He'd come to ENCOM to settle a score in the first place; now he grinned fiercely at the Central Computer Area, where the Master Control Program waited. *C'mon out and fight!*

The Sailer abruptly trembled under them, the first disturbance in her swift maiden voyage. The transmission beam was suddenly brighter, louder, more powerful. The Sailer fought her helm as if she'd come into a squall, her sails cracking. The transmission beam intensified.

Flynn heard running boots on the catwalk and saw Tron charge aft, his face transformed with concern for Yori. Tron didn't bother with a second glance at the transmission beam; he'd seen that it was operating under some guidance. This was no malfunction, but a subversion of the beam; the MCP had taken control of it. Perhaps Master Control had devoted the staggering amount of time and attention necessary to monitor the entire webwork and locate the Sailer. Or—Tron had time for a single searing jolt of guilt—perhaps the MCP had detected his hurl of the disk.

Profitless to consider that now. Tron bounded past Flynn, who was regaining his balance, and was at Yori's side. The transmission beam had risen to a terrifying pitch that nearly drowned out his voice as he shouted to ask her if she was all right. She was, but that was only an instant's relief.

"What's happening?" Flynn hollered over the tumult of the beam and the Sailer's answering tossing and rocking. All of them clutched for handholds to keep from being pitched overboard.

"Power surge!" Yori yelled back. "From the MCP!" She was doing her best to bring the vessel under control. For a moment, Flynn was convinced that he was watching Lora, not an alter ego or simulacrum, but *her*.

Tron steadied her and took in their situation, the insane gyrations of bow and stern, the thrumming of the four lines and the undulations of the great sails. The vessel bucked again and he gripped Yori, shouting over the furor, "We have to get off this beam!"

She'd scanned the readouts, and told him without quaver, "I *can't!* There's no junction due for at least seven or eight nanoseconds!"

The word *junction* caught Flynn's ear as he struggled aft to join them. The Sailer must get off the booby-trapped beam and onto another. He searched, then pointed. "There's another beam!" It glittered in the distance, their salvation. They'd sailed the beam on which they now rode all the way from the Factory Domain, and he'd never seen what transferral entailed. Flynn hoped it was no big deal: *Got a long way to fall,* he reminded himself.

"It's too far!" Yori hollered back. *Which means,* Flynn surmised, *that the Sailer'll either drop out of the sky, explode, or be held fast until the Good Ship Sark shows up.*

He knew a sudden hatred of a scheme of things that could end their mission so. *But we won!* he nearly cried aloud. *Survived that colliseum, the tanks, the Recos, the Reds!* Tron and Yori were close together, she gathered in by the long, muscular arm, both of them resigned.

The game was over, Flynn was concluding, just as an idea occurred to him and his mind finished, *barring the unpredictable Kevin Flynn!*

Tron saw Flynn drag himself upright and sprint toward the Sailer's bow, tossed from rail to rail as he ran. Something in his attitude stopped the User Champion from yelling to him to stay where he was and hold on. The assertion that Flynn was a User was something Tron found easy to doubt at times, but not now. He knew the sudden hope that had come to him in duels on the Game Grid, when he'd thought himself about to die but had found a means to live and win instead. Following Flynn's progress forward, he felt what other User-Believers had felt when they'd watched Tron fight.

"Flynn!" he shouted, but the other kept moving. "What are you doing?" Flynn went on, giving no sign of having heard.

He came to the free-standing steps of the ship's forebody, suppressing his conviction that things like steps had no business hanging in midair, ascending them three at a time. Racing up the companionway, he staggered between the masts and out onto the bow, nearly losing his balance and slipping overboard.

The sails strained and cracked as if before a gale. He teetered past one of the three long antennae that radiated from the hull, now swinging crazily. Through his mind passed all that he knew of his new phantasmagorical World, the behavior of energy there, and what passed for matter. He summoned up memories of his own amazing feats, the sensations when he'd stolen the aura of the downed Red and unconsciously liberated power in the dismantled Reco. He narrowed his concentration to those things; they must guide him now.

He made his way out onto the prow, stopping just short of jutting flanges that guarded the beam-emission aperture like teeth. Flynn readied his will, thought about power, and concentrated on the flow of energy beneath him.

Tron, watching from the helmsman's station, arm around Yori, suddenly understood what Flynn had in mind. The insane audacity of it, and the remote possibility that Flynn might be able to bring it off, made him exclaim, "The beam connection!"

Flynn lay full length on the deck, angling his shoulder around to the gap between the bases of two flanges. The beam flared and sizzled, an outgushing of energy like the lurid mouth of Hell. He rummaged within himself for whatever dormant resource it had been that had permitted him to do the things he had. He extended an arm into the path of the beam. It was not disintegrated; he watched his own splayed fingers within the raging outpouring of power. And he found that he knew precisely what to do.

He thrust his entire arm into the transmission beam as if it were a medium no more dangerous than water. Tron and Yori hiked themselves higher in their seats, trying to see. Flynn pointed his free arm at the other transmission beam he'd spied in the distance. Knowledge came, and control.

From his arm a ray of intolerably bright light projected, nothing less than another transmission beam. It struck and melted with the one in the distance, an improvised link. Flynn felt as if he were about to blow apart, his electronic physiology barely able to cope with the tremendous forces. Tron and Yori watched him, a figure out of a fable, doing a deed without precedent.

"He's creating a junction!" shouted Tron over the din. "Quick; transfer to the other beam!"

Yori resumed her piloting at once. Flynn lay, partially within the beam, slumped and limp. If it hadn't been for his extended arm, Tron would have thought him dead.

The Solar Sailer jarred and came around, slowly at first, then with gathering velocity, riding Flynn's impromptu junction toward safety, swinging free of the beam sabotaged by Master Control. Tron tried not to think what would happen if Flynn suddenly de-rezzed.

But in moments the Sailer, under Yori's helmsmanship, had reached the safe beam and was on a new course, out of danger. Somewhere, Tron thought, the MCP and its slave programs must be very surprised.

Tron ran forward, Yori close behind. He took the forward companionway in two long bounds and was out onto the sloping bow. Flynn lay where he'd been, arm no longer raised. Tron carefully dragged him from the path of the beam emitted from the Sailer's bow, and picked him up. Then he was carrying Flynn back toward the bridge.

Tron set him down gently on the deck, and he and Yori bent over Flynn anxiously, unsure what to do.

But just then Flynn's eyes blinked open. He raised his head, groggy and weak. "Did we make it?"

They sighed their tremendous relief. "Yes," grinned Tron.

Flynn produced a thin, exhausted smile. "Hoo-ray for our side!" Then his head lolled once more; he lost consciousness again. And the transmission beam drove the Solar Sailer on her perilous course toward rendezvous with Master Control.

In time they came to the end of the Game Sea. The colorific ocean halted as its swells confronted a barrier wall so high that it blocked the Sailer's way, so wide that Tron and Yori could see no end to it. But the transmission beam carried them into a gap in the barrier, and over the Central Computer Area.

They were still in the vessel's bridge area, midships. Yori sat with Flynn's head cradled in her lap, watching him. She and Tron could do little for him. She now believed Flynn's claims, she found, even though they seemed impossible and ran counter to everything she knew. His performance on the bow had left no room for doubt.

Yori watched him carefully for any sign of energy loss or instability, or the appearance of scan lines. "Is he de-rezzing?" she solicited Tron's opinion.

"No," posited Tron, who knelt nearby. "But I couldn't tell

you why." There'd been sufficient power in that beam to destroy a thousand programs. Tron, too, found it difficult not to credit Flynn's story now that it had been substantiated so spectacularly.

Flynn stirred out of his senselessness by degrees, finding himself held by Yori, an altogether agreeable situation except that he felt like he'd just spent three days locked inside a cement mixer. Segments of it came back to him as he smiled up at her, thinking it was Lora who cradled his head. Then he remembered everything, and realized that this radiant woman was not the one who'd left him. "Oh, Mommy!" he groaned.

He looked around dizzily. *Still here,* he concluded, *no two ways about that! It's always a pleasure to wake up alive.* "You guys feelin' okay?" he inquired.

Are we— Tron threw his head back and laughed at the nonchalance of it. Yori gave Flynn a fond look, finding that she valued something irreverent and humorous in him. Flynn was not like Tron, but he was stubbornly wry, bravely funny, strong in his own way.

"We are fine," she assured him. "We're worried about you."

Flynn groped himself, still woozy, checking his person for damage and, to his surprise, finding none. "All in one piece," he reported. "Guess I'm still with you."

He sat up and regretted it at once; wincing with pain, he held his head. "Man! Tell the guy with the jackhammer to lay off, will ya?"

Tron chuckled; Flynn seemed all right, apart from that monster headache and strange turn of speech. "How did you do that, Flynn?" he asked, meaning the beam junction.

Flynn looked down at his brilliant Electronic World body, pondering. It had been energy manipulating energy, but the explanation was more complicated than that. A great deal of it had been the instinctive use of the altered structure of his body and the faculties with which he'd been invested by the digitization of that enormously complicated System, his former body.

"Elementary physics," he ad-libbed vaguely. "A beam of energy can always be diverted." He hiked himself up and glanced around curiously, seeking to change the subject. "Are we there yet?"

Yori answered, "Almost. I just have to adjust our course

at the next junction." She began to rise. "I'd better go check the instruments." She gently slid away from him, lithe and marvelous to see.

The Sailer wove among the gigantic canyons of the Central Computer Area, staying at low altitude to avoid detection. The Electronic landscape had a nonlinear, almost weathered look locally. Flynn watched shining palisades, delineated in light and color, roll by to either side. Some time had passed since they'd entered the area, without sign of pursuit. Tron had begun to hope that, in suddenly leaving the transport beam as they had, they'd convinced Sark and the MCP that they'd been destroyed or met their end in a crash.

But that hope vanished an instant later; the Carrier came full speed out of a side canyon just as the Sailer crossed its course.

"Sark!" Tron shouted, even as Yori dove for the controls in a useless effort to avert collision. Flynn wondered wildly what he could possibly do now. The Solar Sailer mounted no weapons, and there was no time or room to maneuver away from the Carrier. Before they could react, the gigantic warship rammed them.

A projecting edge of the Carrier's bow structure sliced into the Sailer as if into a toy. The catwalk was sheared in two, and the great metallic sails collapsed and tore, their masts broken like matchsticks. Her hull moaned and shrieked as if in torment; pieces of the Sailer flew loose to fall, spinning madly.

Yori turned and called Tron's name as Tron, halfway along the catwalk, off to try some last tactic, vanished overboard, knocked from the craft by the collision. They heard his brief cry, "Flynn!" fading as he fell. Yori and Flynn were thrown against one another and flung to the deck.

Flynn could do nothing but hold Yori and try to keep her from falling too. Given time, he might have been able to summon up his strange abilities, but there was none. He clutched frantically at some wreckage, clinging to Yori, unable to do anything else. The gaping maw of an open hold or hangar in the Carrier's bow raced toward them.

Half of the Sailer's forebody dropped away. The remainder of it, a last island of flotsam bearing Flynn and Yori, was swallowed up by the Carrier a moment later.

Chapter Fifteen

DUMONT TURNED AS the cell door opened, ready for death.

He was convinced that even Sark must have tired of tormenting him and the other older programs who were captives aboard the Carrier. It was beyond his power to resist or object, and so he stood, resigned. But instead of taking Dumont from the cell, the guards thrust into it Yori, and another program Dumont didn't recognize.

Dumont was shocked and sorry; he'd hoped that Yori and Tron had escaped, perhaps even held some chance of saving the System.

Yori rushed to Dumont with a sob, and he sadly took her in his arms. Flynn stood dejectedly by the cell door, shoulders drooping in defeat. He recognized Dumont and saw the metamorphosis the old program had undergone, but spared little attention for him. Flynn's disk had been taken from him by the guards who'd surrounded and boarded the wreckage of the Sailer the instant it had come to rest in the Carrier's hold; the fight had been brief.

The sound of Yori's crying tore at Flynn. "Tron?" Dumont asked her. Flynn looked away from them then, to lean glumly against the wall.

"He's dead," she answered, scarcely audible.

Dumont sighed, the last of his hope truly gone. He looked

151

to Flynn, curious by long habit rather than real impulse. "And who is this?"

"He's a User, Dumont," Yori told him. "He came to our World—trying to help us. Tron believed in him." Flynn thought better of correcting her misimpression. It just didn't matter, and he had no wish to add to her disillusionment. Yori's voice had broken with that last, and she turned her face from the erstwhile Guardian.

But Dumont was studying Flynn, uncertain whether or not to credit what she'd said. "If the Users can no longer help us—" He was unable to finish the thought. The System was forever the MCP's.

Suddenly, light came up to full intensity in the cell; they all looked to the door. Through it came Sark, filled with an appalling glee. He swept them with his stare, saying, "So, we have erased the program that—"

He stopped as his eye fell on Flynn. When he'd been informed of the capture of the Sailer's crew, he'd assumed the other program to be of no significance, since he wasn't Tron. But now his eyes widened in disbelief. "You! No!"

He'd never seen Flynn close-up, and thought now that Clu had somehow returned from oblivion. "You were de-rezzed," thundered Sark, "I saw you!"

Flynn looked him over, the tall figure in elaborate armor and vaned casque-helmet, the Dillinger face which now held surprise and confusion, and even a touch of fear.

Flynn smirked, not sure what Sark meant, but quick to play the debonair ghost. "That's never stopped me before."

Sark reasserted control over himself. "Well, we can take care of that soon enough." After all, the program had been captured and confined, proving that he had no supernatural powers. This time Sark would see to it that the job was done properly.

He pointed to Dumont and a trio of guards grabbed the old Guardian.

"Take that program to the holding pit," Sark commanded, and they began to haul Dumont from the cell.

Yori rushed to intervene, crying, "Dumont!" But one of the guards shoved her back. Flynn's anger suddenly flared, but he thought better of a fight in those surroundings. *My time'll come,* he simmered.

Sark turned his despising gaze on them, his confidence buoyed by the ease with which he'd had her brutalized. Indicating Dumont, who waited with a pained, stoic expression, Sark told the others, "I'm taking our friends here, and some other religious fanatics, to Master Control. The MCP has expressed an interest in assimilating them, probably for archival purposes. I'm not going back to the Game Grid on this ship, though."

Flynn heard it uncertainly, not sure why the Command Program was telling them all this. That sadistic smile transformed Sark's face once more. "I'll take the transport beam. But when I disembark, this ship and everything that remains on board will automatically de-rezz." He looked to Flynn. "This means you."

Yori gasped and Flynn could find no rejoinder. Sark roared with evil mirth, turning to go, the guards and Dumont following. On the upper level of the brig section Sark paused to look down into the holding pit where other captives, benumbed, waited submissively. They were aged and weak, their lives had been leeched away. There were a dozen of them, former Tower Guardians like Dumont, whose function had been abolished by the MCP along with belief in the Users, and freedom of the System. The Command Program watched with approval as the door opened below and more guards went in to herd the enervated, unprotesting programs forth, manhandling them.

Flynn glanced up as he heard boots tramp by overhead, to see Sark through the cell's transparent ceiling.

Sark took pleasure in the glare of resentment and fury that Flynn gave him. Flynn watched Sark go off, finding no way in which he could get even or avenge Ram and Crom, unable to think of a way of saving Yori. He wondered with foreboding what being de-rezzed would feel ilke.

The Carrier made its approach to the Central Processing Unit, which stood like a huge, computer-modeled mesa in the middle of the Central Computer Area. It was, on the scale of the System, miles across, perfectly flat, carpeted with circuitry meshwork, its level smoothness broken only by the huge metallic cylinder that was the citadel of the MCP. A Communication Beam reached down from on high, passing directly through the rotating saw-toothed band of the focusing antenna, to strike the center of the citadel's roof. A halo of free data bits orbited the citadel like an asteroid belt. Information flowed unendingly in this heart of Master Control's empire; lesser beams were arriving constantly, to hit the relay prisms set around the citadel and be deflected toward the MCP.

Aboard the Carrier, Sark's lieutenant saluted him, saying, "Docking module prepared to disengage, sir." Sark entered the docking module with his lieutenant while his guards drove Dumont and the other Guardians aboard. The lieutenant stepped to the control bank, preparing the shuttlecraft for departure while Sark stared down at the citadel through the craft's observation pane. His pleasure in his victory would have been diminished had he been aware of the tiny figure clinging grimly to the outer hull of his Carrier, working its way with cautious haste toward the module.

A beam flared from the CPU mesa, touching the Carrier just beneath its bridge, a guidance and command from the MCP. Sark personally engaged the control to initiate separation. The module, a part of the Carrier's bridge structure, began to slide free of its slotted docking niche.

"Intermediate vectors detached," the lieutenant reported, eyes to his readouts.

"Route us to the MCP," Sark ordered, eyes fixed on the citadel. "I want to get rid of this dead weight and catch a transport beam back to the Game Domain."

The docking pod, disengaged, lifted smoothly from the bulk of the Carrier, rising clear of it then reorienting for descent to the mesa. It picked up velocity, bound for the brilliant metal cylinder. And with the shuttle, clinging to its side with hands and feet wedged with desperate strength against the sides of the hull slot where he'd lodged himself, Tron wondered if he could keep his grip long enough to reach the MCP and work his revenge.

Yori sat, despondent, head in hands, unable to bring herself to believe that Tron was dead. He had returned to her after so much peril and adversity that it was hard not to expect him to do so again. But she kept telling herself that it did no good to keep playing images of him in her head, or longing for him. He was gone, and she soon would be. She knew a lassitude like that she'd felt as an automaton worker in the Factory Domain, uncaring of what was to come.

Not so, Flynn. He was at the door of the cell, feeling its frame methodically, testing its edges for weakness or access to its locking mechanism. He'd made one hurried search, in case there'd been hope of quick release, but had located none and was now forcing himself to go over the same ground again, slowly, alert for the slightest irregularity or feature, anything that might spell survival.

He looked to Yori and thought about asking her to help, but she was sunk in mourning and he decided that trying to persuade her would only waste precious time. He went back to his probings, aware that time was against him.

The docking module settled in over the mountainous Central Processing Unit. It lowered easily into a docking niche, its hull protuberances sliding into the keyways there. Sark placed a palm over another control sensor. The entire bulkhead before him rose and swung completely away to reveal the wide, flat vista of the CPU. Far off across the mesa was the citadel, a great, glittering cylinder with vertical, bladelike flanges around its circumference.

With the docking module no longer in it, its assignment complete, the Carrier swung away from its holding station, its control systems already failing as it began to de-rezz. Unlike those of many other simulations and all programs in the System as run by the MCP, the Carrier's structure was stored for duplication.

Flynn, still exploring the door, felt its substance alter and begin to fade, and yelled, "Hey!" Recalling what Sark had said about the Carrier's de-rezzing, he began to hope. If the process took place slowly enough, there might be a way to get out of this. He turned to Yori.

She'd looked up when he'd called out, but evinced no interest in what was happening to the door, no change in the lethargic surrender into which she'd sunk. Flynn went to her and knelt by her side.

"Yori," he implored, "I still have power. Sark doesn't know that." If he could just keep some substance to the ship for a little while, they stood a chance. *I've gotta,* he told himself. He took her arm to pull her up, to save her with or without her volition. Leaving her behind was out of the question; it would've been abandoning Lora.

But she fought his grip, resisting any new conflict, even a struggle to live, choosing to remain in her grief and numbness. "No!" she grimaced, twisting away. "Leave me alone! We've failed!"

He seized both her hands, shaking her. "We only fail if we give up trying! Come on!"

He released her and rushed back to the door, hoping she would follow. He pressed his hands in among the dispersing obstacle of the door, feeling the weird tickle of the interplaying scan lines as it continued to de-rezz. There *was* a chance! "Look," he exclaimed, facing her again, "the door's almost—"

He stopped, aghast. Yori stood unmoving, looking down at her hands. And Flynn saw that Sark hadn't overlooked the fate of his captives; Yori was de-rezzing too. Her body was becoming transparent, undergoing conversion to nonexistence, and for her there would be no restoration. She gazed blankly at herself, then to Flynn, as she lost substance.

Flynn hurried to her, taking her in his arms and holding her close, willing her to live. He opened himself to the flow of those powers he only half understood. Her lids drooped and nearly closed and she felt weightless, ethereal. Flynn channeled all his determination into the thought that she mustn't leave him.

Energy was imparted to her by Flynn. "Yori!" he pleaded, half a sob. He bent closer to her, their lips separated only by the smallest of spaces. The energy flow became a torrent, with the dynamics of his emotion.

Suddenly her eyes opened wider, and wider still, revealing her astonishment. She gazed up at him, dumbfounded. Color and substance passed into her, and the torpor gave way to animation. Flynn pulled back from her a little, treating himself to the matchless sight of Yori restored. She had trouble finding the words. "You—you brought me back? Why? *How?*"

He remembered that there was no time to lose, none for the many things he wanted to say. "I'm gonna need your help," he told her. "Let's get outta here!" He took her hand, and they fled.

* * *

The line of woebegone prisoners shuffled along the path
to the MCP, shepherded by stern Memory Guards. At their
head marched Sark, holding his pace down so that he didn't
outdistance the depleted Guardians. The transplendent citadel
of the MCP rose before them. Sark was content; all things in
the System were as they should be, as Master Control decreed
them. Sark intended to see that they stayed that way.

Forever.

Back at the docking module, Sark's lieutenant stood a
relaxed guard. There was nothing to fear here—unless one
were on the wrong side of the MCP's temper—but leaving a
sentry with the craft was standard procedure. The lieutenant
looked forward to a period of leisure and entertainment when
they returned to the Game Grid; there would be plenty of
competitors for the Command Program to match himself
against, plenty of prisoners to use up in the grand combats
of the arena. That would be fine, something to enjoy.

The lieutenant heard the smallest of noises, the passage of
something keen-edged and fearsomely fast dividing the air.
He barely had time to turn before a disk smashed him with its
fiery discharge, flinging him backward off his feet. His body
de-rezzed at once as the disk whirled back through the air
to its master.

Tron stepped out of the pod's shadow, hurdling what was
left of the de-rezzing officer, and started off after the line of
prisoners. He had only caught hold of the projection on the
Carrier's hull, the one that had saved his life after the collision, by chance and desperate flailing, to watch wreckage
from the Sailer fall past him. Hatred had given him the endurance to pull himself along the hull.

When the Carrier had settled in toward the Central Processing Unit, Tron, knowing Sark's preferences, had anticipated
his next move. The ponderous Carrier wouldn't set down;
Sark would descend in his shuttle and return to the Game
Grid by transport beam. And so Tron had raced time,
clambering across the ship's hull, limbs straining with the
effort, to reach the docking pod before it launched from the
Carrier for good. Only an unswerving commitment to carrying out Alan-One's plan and destroying the MCP had kept
Tron from jumping Sark as soon as the pod had grounded.
But that would have forewarned the MCP of Tron's presence,
and so revenge on Sark would have to come in its own time.

Tron picked up his pace, reducing the prisoner file's lead, moving cautiously but quickly.

The prisoners marched despondently down the grade of bare mesa surface and began up the slight incline leading to the entrance of the citadel, heads hung in surrender. The sad procession was lit, as if with heat lightning, by the incessant beams entering and leaving the place as the MCP kept constant, jealous watch over all activities and events in its realm.

Sark, watching it all with pleasure, brought a heavy, gauntleted hand down on Dumont's shoulder as the old Guardian went by. "Come on, Dumont," he said. "Soon it'll all be over." Not meaning Dumont alone, of course; soon the MCP's control over the System—over all Systems—would end freedom, end the useful functioning of programs, end anything but what the Master Control Program chose to permit.

The decrepit programs, their feet dragging, came in before the MCP. Up it towered above them, a hundred feet high and more, a cylinder, its surface reflective, burnished and hard, covered with patterns of circuitry and light. And stretched across that surface, a convex grotesquerie, was the face of the MCP. It gazed down at them with eyes that seemed blind, but saw all. Its visage was an eerie combination of the slack, swollen features of an idiot with those of a shrewd, malicious demon spirit. It was a bloated apparition that knew it was such, willed itself to be so, and used that appearance. Just then, the face was colored in luminous pastels.

The MCP's circular base was supported by an inverted cone of light. That cone rested, in turn, upon another, upright cone, which radiated from the citadel's floor, sharing its vertex. Master Control stared down, relishing the old Guardians' defeated look. At the guards' rough promptings, the old programs ranged out along the curved wall of the MCP's lair, eyes downcast, waiting, acquiescent.

The MCP's thick, loose lips moved. "WELCOME!" The word was heavy with irony, rolling through the place at enormous volume, echoing and distorted, hurting their ears.

Sark crossed to Dumont who, by defying him, had earned the first place among the scheduled executions. He took the unprotesting Guardian in a grip that brooked no resistance and forced him back, throwing him against the concave wall behind him. Dumont was immediately spread against the wall and pinned to it by the MCP's power, held firm in an anguished pose, face contorted by suffering. One by one the other programs were whisked backward by the MCP's invisible grasp, sharing Dumont's agony.

A slow, careful de-rezzing began, the Master Control Program searching within the Guardians for those components it wished to retain, prolonging their suffering. Its spectral, overwhelming voice shook the citadel.

"Programs! You are participating in the creation of the single most powerful program in the history of the System—of *all* Systems!"

A Guardian faded from existence, then another. Those remaining were beginning to grow indistinct as they were devoured by the ever-ravenous MCP. Dumont wished that he could hurl some last defiance, but he hadn't the strength.

"An entity with a will!" the MCP boasted. "With ambition! A *superior form of life!*"

Chapter Sixteen

No one else was left aboard the Carrier. Flynn didn't think they'd been put down elsewhere; they'd been callously abandoned by Sark, to de-rezz.

Yori knew the location of the bridge from her work in the Factory Domain. They ran for their lives down the passageways and ladderwells of the de-rezzing vessel.

They emerged into the soaring emptiness of the bridge, stopping where Sark had once stood to survey the Domains and command the ship. They spared only a quick look at the enigmatic mesa of the CPU. "Check out the controls," Flynn bade Yori, knowing that there was no time for him to experiment.

She moved at once to the main console, studying it and drawing on her memories of the Factory Complex. "We're getting closer," Flynn warned as the ship drifted toward the MCP's citadel. He could see portions of the great hull de-rezzing, leaving only a ghostly outline. The process was proceeding quickly; he tried urgently to come up with their next move. Even with his power, he doubted that he could stabilize the structure of such an enormous object, much less reverse the de-rezzing. But perhaps, he thought, the Carrier would last long enough to allow them a crack at the MCP.

Right now, that was all Flynn wanted.

Dumont was disappearing slowly, his body a blizzard of de-rezzing, the fight having all but left him.

"You thought you could resist me, Dumont," Master Control gloated in its loathsome voice. "But I won. I outclassed you!"

Dumont became fainter yet. Sark watched it with much enthusiasm, but heard a catch in the MCP's voice, as if the next taunt had been held back. "Wait! Sark!" it snapped. Sark jumped, coming to full alert. "I feel a presence," Master Control said slowly, evaluating the data that had attracted its attention. "A Warrior?" it queried itself.

Sark was saved anxious questions; the single word rang out behind him, sharp and resonant, edged with anger. "Sark!"

He spun to see Tron waiting, his blue circuitry brilliant with hatred and the thirst for vengeance.

The User Champion stood poised for battle, disk in hand. The disk gave off a peculiar, pure light, like nothing Sark had seen before, one which touched off disturbing uncertainties in him. Wearing a look of unmixed hatred, Tron stood outside the entrance to the citadel, inviting combat. Sark thrust aside doubts, moving toward him, reaching for his own disk.

"I don't know how you survived, slave," Sark shouted, lip curled, emerging from the citadel. "Prepare to terminate!"

He cast his disk with a powerful sweep of his arm, an expert throw. The weapon flickered across the gap between them in an instant, but Tron contrived to drop to one knee just in time, and lean aside, and it passed by overhead. The disk circled, rising, but instead of homing to the Command Program's hand it dove at Tron once more. This time Tron met it with upraised disk; the two weapons clashed with an outpouring of light of unbearable intensity.

Sark's disk sprang away from the encounter, cleaving the air on its return course, seeking its master's grip. At it went, Tron gathered himself for a counterattack of his own. Sark's eyes were alight at having his first attack countered, his mouth twisted into a line of fury. "You are very persistent, Tron!" he grated.

Tron's weapon came at him; it ricocheted from Sark's up-lifted disk, soared, and stooped for him a second time. Again it was repulsed by the Command Program, and Sark immediately cast at Tron as Tron's disk raced back to its owner in response to his urgent summons. The two missiles of light cut the air, nearly side by side. Tron waited, braced, aware that his cast had expended much of its energy while Sark's was fresh.

"I'm also better than you," he answered Sark's derision, and suited action to words. At the last moment, his disk rose above Sark's and Tron launched himself into the air, pulling his legs up under him. Sark's disk whisked by underneath, making a deadly sound, and Tron plucked his own from the air.

He landed nimbly, hearing the angry scream of the Command Program's weapon as it banked for another try at him. Tron judged his response by the sound; he pivoted, bringing up his disk at just the right angle, rigid arms extended. Sark's weapon hit Tron's full-on with extreme violence and rebounded with a splashing explosive brilliance. Then Tron spun to meet the next assault.

"Yori! Yori! Look!"

In the drifting Carrier, Flynn had spotted the lightning-battle of the duel. He couldn't escape the feeling that he'd looked down on *one* of those Warriors, from a similar angle, from the heights of the Game Grid.

Yori, staring where Flynn pointed, reacted with a piercing, thankful cry, *"Tron!"* He'd been given back to her; by what fates, she never questioned. She ignored her dilemma, unable to do anything but watch the deadly contest; Flynn, too, was transfixed.

Tron waited, balance distributed carefully, tensed. Sark hurled again, a blurringly fast release. It covered the distance between them in an instant, but Tron managed to deflect, and counterreleased. Sark had recalled his own weapon, mocking, "Very clever, Tron." He deflected, as Tron had.

Tron's disk homed to him and they stood awaiting one another's moves for a moment, each sizing up the most formidable enemy he'd ever met, each wondering how long the fragile pause would last.

"You should have joined me," jeered Sark.

Tron concluded that a reply would be a waste of time. Sark would never understand how everything that had happened underscored and reinforced Tron's commitment to the Users. Then something high above caught his eye and he looked up, though he knew it might be some trick; he had to risk a glance, to insure that he wasn't being threatened from another quarter. Then he spotted the derelict Carrier.

It should have vanished, he knew. There was only one individual who might have delayed that, even slightly: Flynn. Tron thought he could see, through the blurring of the intangible outline of the ship, figures standing within the remaining portion of the bridge. *And Yori?* He let himself hope.

Sark noticed Tron's distraction. Though the Command Program wasn't sure what this delayed de-rezzing of his vessel might mean, he took quick advantage of Tron's divided attention, snap-pitching his weapon with all his might. He'd seen for himself the formidable power of Tron's altered disk and wanted to end the contest quickly, in any way he could. But the sound and movement brought Tron back to himself; he crouched and brought up his disk again, bracing arms and shoulders, preparing for the vicious collision, concentrating on angles and speed.

Again there was the coruscating shock of contact, again the deflection.

As Sark's disk shrieked back to its master, Tron wound and cast. He put behind it all the might of his arm, and incorporated all the finesse he'd acquired in the arena. He used a unique variation; Sark had not yet felt the full power of Tron's disk as refurbished by Alan-One.

Sark caught his disk on its return only to see Tron's headed directly for him. The Command Program held up his blue weapon to shield himself again, confident, wondering when, as must inevitably happen, Tron's endurance or skill would flag. "We would have made a great team!" he mocked.

But Tron's disk did a roll on its course, drawing Sark's guard off, to continue its flight vertically, edge on, its angle of attack abruptly altered. There was a detonation as it met its red opposition, the failure of Sark's defense. Tron's disk sheared through it, sundering it, shattering it in Sark's hands, passing through the casque-helmet and cleaving a path of ruin through the helmet's contents.

Sark stood, empty hands still uplifted, eyes bulging in shock and disbelief, face slack. An instant later, energy and the essence of the program Sark began to gush from the hideous wound like smoking, phosphorescent blood, roiling and crackling, streaming down his face and armor, evaporating off into the air.

Tron recaught his disk and watched his enemy without pity. Sark stood unmoving for a moment, then toppled, pitching face-first to the ground. The User Champion glided past the fallen Command Program, headed for the entrance to the citadel.

The MCP sensed someone coming, made its assumption, and boomed, "Good, Sark!"

Tron stepped into the entrance. "I don't think it *is* good for you, MCP," he told it in a level tone.

The voice of the MCP was mountainous in its anger. "Sark!" it called, its eerie, distorted eyes searching the entrance for its Champion. "How have you allowed this program to—"

"Sark's out!" shouted Tron, cutting through the rantings of the MCP.

"SARK!" it persisted. Tron, looking for the Memory Guards, saw that they'd fled, unwilling to face the Champion who'd destroy the mighty Sark. The MCP's face shone in fiery reds.

Tron spotted Dumont against the wall, nearly gone into the cessation of de-rezzing. He raced to Dumont's side and the MCP's face seemed to follow him, sliding around the wall of the cylinder to keep him under surveillance. Tron made a futile attempt to pull Dumont from the wall. It was useless. "Dumont!"

Dumont mustered a last iota of strength. "No, Tron. Must destroy—MCP first."

Tron shouted, trying to keep the old Guardian focused. "Dumont! Where's Yori? Where's Flynn?"

He could barely hear Dumont's answer. "Left on the Carrier—erased." *No, not yet!* Tron knew; a portion of the craft still endured. But the MCP had to be dealt with first, or everything else would be in vain.

He spun, eyes flashing, pulling back for the cast. "Program!

Stop!" ordered the MCP. "This is not allowed!" It had come
to an unthinkable situation, in real danger of being terminated. It devoted a tremendous amount of its attention to
trying to locate its Champion and summon him.

Tron let fly; the disk hit the Master Control Program's
gleaming surface with a blinding release of power. The
MCP's protective panels swung into place around its supporting cones as its crimson face wailed in a stupendous
voice, *"Sark!"*

Out on the mesa, Sark lay motionless. But the MCP had
located him now. Energy began to converge along the circuitry contours, coalescing around the inert form, concentrating. The gutted shell that had been Sark could no longer
function as a complete program; indeed, it hadn't de-rezzed
already only because of safeguards and the enormous power
allocated the Command Program by the MCP. And those
were nearly gone.

But the remaining body would respond to the MCP's
direct commands, given sufficient power. And power the
MCP sent it, spendthrift in its fear of Tron. Energy swarmed
to Sark's corpse; it began to stir.

Tron threw his disk at the panels over and over, with
blazing impact, determined to break down its defenses and
eliminate it from the System forever, urgent in his need to
save Yori and Flynn and Dumont.

"SARRRKKK!" howled the MCP.

And out on the mesa, obedient to the command, coronaed
with the incredible amount of energy it had required to
animate it, the mutilated body of Sark rose once more. Still
more power sluiced into him. The MCP could only survive
by making a zombie of the Command Program's body,
funneling into it sufficient energy to run half a Domain, no
miser when it came to survival. Sark's corpse expanded,
grew.

High above, Yori saw the bright, unholy resurrection.
"Flynn, look!"

Sark was a giant now, his eyes a vacant, burnt-out white-
on-white. The hole in his helmet and skull was as before;
the horrible wound gaped. He moved toward the entrance of
the citadel with lurching, clumsy strides, but each movement spoke of invincible might.

That would be all she wrote, Flynn saw. He'd been elated

to see Tron win, had swapped hugs with Yori and waited to watch the MCP go up like a roman candle. But even Tron, Flynn sensed, could not stand before this final manifestation of the MCP's evil. Flynn looked back to the citadel, with its communication beam descending directly to its center, and thought of a plan.

"Yori, steer us over by the beam, right next to it!"

She went to the controls, striving to harness what little propulsion the derelict had left. "How will that help?"

Flynn started for the passageway, making for what remained of the outer hull. Sark's corpse was stomping toward the MCP. Flynn called back to her, "I'm going to jump." He sized up the beam, trying to calculate his leap—for life?

She stared at him with her mouth open. *Maybe these wild talents of mine will work. If I can enter the MCP, I might be able to do something. Only way to fail's not to try; only way to find out is the old Geronimo!* Flynn thought.

Tron fired off his disk once more as the Master Control Program's panels spun to spread the impact and energy discharges. Tron prepared for another toss. Just then a heart-stopping, demonic roar brought him around.

Tron stood frozen by the sight. Sark was a colossus, wreathed in power, still bearing the ghastly wound. The horror of it daunted even the User Champion.

"TRON!" The bellow was uttered in a voice that combined many, with Sark's and the MCP's foremost among them, as if uncounted prisoner programs now inhabited Sark.

Overcoming his moment's irresolution, Tron coiled, let fly. The disk left a trail of white luminance in the air, a perfect throw. And yet the huge creature reached forth a hand and deflected it easily with his palm. Tron recalled the disk, circling to one side, despairing, but unwilling to give up.

The Carrier closed on the beam at a tortuous crawl, all but spent. Flynn stood on the edge of the superstructure, looking down at it as Yori watched in complete consternation.

"Flynn, you can't" she declared. "You'll be de-rezzed!"

He turned to her, placing a finger to her lips. *So much like Lora!* "Probably," he confessed. He took her into an embrace, bent close to her. She stared at him, uncomprehending but trusting. This time, their lips met. The kiss was a new experience for Yori, but she apprehended, right away, what it was. She responded in kind.

Yori's body became radiant once more, its aura brightening as it had in the apartment. She was filled with feelings she couldn't sort out or analyze, an affection for Flynn that was unlike her love of Tron, but undeniable, and wonderful. She transformed once more, the circuitry giving way to traceries, and was gossamer-winged in her mantle, hair flowing freely, her eyes closed in rapture.

Flynn pulled back to take in the sight of her, enthralled. A moment later her eyes opened. "Don't worry," Flynn whispered. He released her and she watched him, unspeaking, wordless with the thing that had happened to her.

Flynn poised on the edge of the fading Carrier, gathered himself, and jumped off the brink, into the MCP's Communication Beam. Yori was at the rail in a swirl of mantle, grief and fear changing her face, to peer after him.

Flynn dropped in a slow-motion dive through the almost physical resistance of the beam, maneuvering himself down the fountain of energy into the heart of the Master Control Program. Yori mourned him no less than she had Tron.

"END OF LINE, PROGRAM," the body of Sark intoned in its multitude of voices, the mockery of Sark and the MCP prominent among them. Tron, heaving for breath, his best attacks ineffective, dodged between the giant's feet. Nearby, Master Control watched with its placid, idiot-feral gaze.

Flynn, arms upraised, slid feet first down the beam, body aglow with his own power. There was an incandescent flash and a feeling like that in the laser lab, when he'd been digitized, of an alteration in his body structure. Then Flynn was inside the very core of the MCP cylinder, where the MCP had never expected or provided against any other entity's intrusion.

Sark's zombie looked up sharply, aware of an unspeakable wrongness. Tron couldn't help but follow the stare, trick or no. The bloated face of the MCP had been replaced by Flynn's distorted, convex features on the wall of the cylinder. Tron had the impression of enormous contention, a battle

of titans within the MCP. He turned to the thing that had
been Sark, but the creature was still absorbed by events within
the cylinder. Perhaps, Tron thought, some indirect attack
on it—

Then he saw the blades protecting the MCP's light cones
swing open, exposing the supporting cones to attack. *Flynn's
doing!* Tron knew.

He readied his disk again and it attracted the corpse's
attention. Tron cast a final time, but not at the hideous thing
that fought him. The disk hissed to circle the vertex where
the energy cones rested one upon the other, supporting the
MCP. The disk maneuvered to Tron's command; it sliced
directly into the vertex.

The citadel resounded to an explosion that nearly rocked
Tron off his feet, the heat of it making him throw his arms
up protectively, the light of it threatening his vision. The
Sark-thing stared at it and the outcry of multitudes came
a last time, "NOOOO!" as it realized what Tron had done.
As it gazed up at the hurricane of energy liberated from the
cones, its eyes were again for a moment those of the real
Sark, stunned with the knowledge that he'd lost irrevocably.

Then the giant became a column of mottled light, losing
all features, seeming to fold in and melt upon itself, dissipating all that had animated it, in a foam of iridescent explosions. Tron stared at it in dreadful fascination, then returned
his gaze to the cylinder.

A new form was coming into being in the madness of
contending powers that threatened the energy cones. It
reminded Tron of Dumont as he had been configured in
his pod, its face ancient, drawn with age, wizened and
emaciated, its pod an earlier and eroded version of a
Guardian's.

High up there, the MCP was losing its fight; it had assumed
this appearance, stripped of the power and accumulations
of its long rise. It looked down through weakened eyes, old
and debilitated. Before it, its gnarled and withered hands
played on an old-fashioned, standard typewriter keyboard,
an instrument from the days of its earliest origins. As Dumont
had predicted: *He started out small, and he'll end up small.*
The face sank backward and down out of the headpiece,
leaving only a dark aperture.

The figure faded from view and the great cylinder of the MCP shone more and more harshly. Tron took a step back, sensing that some final finish was yet to come. Along the wall, the figures of Dumont and the other Guardians were rezzing up, their substance and essence released from the destroying Master Control. Tron took Dumont by the arm, gesturing to the others, urging them from the citadel.

Detonation after detonation blossomed across the surface of the MCP, licking out at the heels of the fleeing programs. They got through the doorway just as the vertical flange panels began to blast free, searing the air and making the floor jolt. The explosions continued, rising around the cylinder, consuming it, eating toward its core.

At last the MCP went up in a sunburst that climbed into the night sky as Yori watched from the drifting Carrier. With that, the surrounding Domains, darkened during the reign of the MCP, began to return to life. The impenetrable sky, blocked off by the influence of Master Control, was once more open to the night; stars and nebulae and comets and moons flashed and winked.

The fireball of the MCP's last eruption climbed, as more Domains revivified in every direction, a carpet of light rolling out to all sides as a ripple expands across a pool from the dropping of a stone. Yori shielded her eyes from the glare of the nova but watched the returning Domains, ecstatic.

The Carrier was descending, little left to it but the bridge area where she stood, its de-rezzing barely halted in time. Below her she saw Tron waving, running across the mesa to reach the spot where the Carrier would touch down.

He gazed up at it, a ghost ship except for the bridge. He doubted that the System would see the ominous flagship again. Yori came to the edge of the bridge as it settled to the ground and jumped the last few feet, into his arms. She was again attired as a worker.

Tron gathered her in happily, laughing, about to welcome her and tell her how dear she was to him. But before he could, she threw her arms around his neck and kissed him full on the mouth, holding it for a long moment, pressing him to her. Surprised at first, he accepted, then savored it. When she released him, he was a little breathless. "Nice!" he panted.

She giggled. "It's something the Users do."

Whatever it was, Tron wasn't sure he liked the idea of her doing it with anyone else, User or not. But that was beside the point right now. He scanned the bridge behind her. "Where's Flynn?" He had a feeling he already knew.

Her face went somber. "He's gone. Into the MCP's beam. He saved you. He saved us, after all."

He looked to where the beam had probed down from the sky and wondered if Flynn had made it home. The events since Flynn's appearance on the scene would take much consideration, Tron thought, much meditation. They had meanings to yield. "So," he murmured, "he really was a User."

A small green meteor swept down past him on a close fly-by, spikes protruding. "Yes!" assured the Bit, who'd finally caught up with his program's friends.

Dumont joined them, and they all watched the System return to life and light, and the sky show the splendor of the stars once more. *How wonderful it must be in his World*, thought Tron. *Thank you, Flynn!* Yori sent a silent message upward.

Chapter Seventeen

FLYNN'S DISEMBODIED POINT of view watched the circuit landscape of the Electronic World draw away from him, growing small at breathtaking speed—except that he had no breath. Soon it had resolved into a globe of intricate geometric shapes limned in light. Then it shrank into infinite distance.

He only half-remembered now the terrific fight with the MCP, in which he'd been aided by Tron's timely inspiration in hurling his disk at the vertex of the energy cones. His instinctive use of his special powers had helped him in his effort to set things to rights, and to direct a reversal of his digitization. And in that he had been aided too by programs that had begun running after the destruction of the MCP. He hoped he hadn't blown it . . .

The laser array hummed, issuing a line of coherent light. It flashed at an exact range, precisely decoding the structure of Flynn's body, a task which would've been impossible if the MCP hadn't devoted so much effort to digitizing him in the first place.

He barely had time to catch his breath, to wonder, to rejoice and raise thanks to the Powers That Be. He barely had

171

time to marvel at the things that had happened to him and think: *Good-bye; good luck!* to his friends.

Because just then the computer began printing out hard copy:

```
file = DSKI:FLYNN .MEM 700,706
- - - - - - - - - - - - - - - - - - - - - - - - - - - - - - - - -
 .dir (flynn) /hist/ listall


File System Accounting Log
Directory Access History
User name:   Kevin O. Flynn
Password:    ★FLOTILLA★
Subdirectory: game software


Access control:
  This User:   encryption protection (level 5)
  Other Users: access denied


Access History:
  File name  Project name      File Created        Last Access


  PARA      "Space Paranoids"   21–MAR by FLYNN   30–AUG by DILLINGER
  VICE      "Vice Squad"        15–APR by FLYNN   30–AUG by DILLINGER
  LITE      "Light Cycles"      10–JUN by FLYNN   30–AUG by DILLINGER
  CIRCMAS   "Circuit Masters"   29–MAR by FLYNN   30–AUG by DILLINGER
  WARP      "Warp Factor"       12–AUG by FLYNN   30–AUG by DILLINGER
```

Flynn snatched up the copy with a whoop and a laugh, and dashed off to find Alan and Lora.

In the aerie of the ENCOM tower, early-morning light grayed the windows of Edward Dillinger's office. He'd spent the night in the sumptuous private suite that adjoined his office, too tired for a limousine or helicopter ride home, only to be awakened in the predawn by an alarm squeal from his desk.

Now he sat before it and watched as one of the desk's many screens showed him the same information that had been printed out for Flynn. There would be no way to hide it now, he knew, nor any way to refile it under limited access. The Master Control Program was no longer running, as if it had been utterly destroyed—by what means, he had no idea. And Bradley's Tron program was running.

Dillinger's superdesk told him that Flynn and the others

were already manipulating the ENCOM system. Soon enough, Gibbs and the rest would be down on Dillinger's neck. His career over, the criminal implications of what he'd done only now coming through to him, he ignored the coming of daylight in the moribund silence of his office.

The black executive helicopter circled down from the blue sky toward the landing pad on the roof of the ENCOM building. Lora and Alan squinted into the blades' backwash as a ground crewman held the chopper's door open.

Out jumped Flynn; grinning broadly, he'd just returned from concluding a major multinational agreement much in ENCOM's favor. He had on a natty double-breasted suit, but had chosen to wear his running shoes.

Y'know, those two don't look too bad together, he thought, as Alan and Lora ran to meet him. He hoisted his attaché case in triumph. When they'd exchanged greetings, Alan said, "Dillinger wants to talk to you; he says it's all a mistake." He had to yell to be heard over turning rotors.

ENCOM's new Senior Operating Officer smirked. A number of lettered agencies were lined up, indictments in hand, for a crack at Edward Dillinger. Flynn shook his head. "Can't; bad for the corporate image." Alan smiled, somewhat like a wolf.

They fell in behind him as Flynn headed for the elevator. "Besides," he finished, "I'm beat."

"Hey," Lora protested, "you've got an executive board meeting."

Flynn turned his smile on them both again; Alan's arm around her shoulders seemed the most appropriate thing in the world. He slipped them a wink. "This *is* the executive board meeting!"

High over the System soared the Solar Sailer, cruising above the glittering beauty of the radiant Domains and the phosphorescent tides of the Game Sea.

Tron stood on the bridge with his arm around Yori. The Sailer changed transmission beams and came onto another tack as the Bit shot past them, playing and cutting figure eights, zipping along next to the graceful Sailer, over a System ablaze, a free System.

ABOUT THE AUTHOR

Brian Daley was born in rural New Jersey in 1947 and currently lives at no fixed address. After an army hitch and the usual odd jobs, he enrolled in college, where he began his first novel. He is the author of *The Doomfarers of Coramonde* and *The Starfollowers of Coramonde*, as well as the Han Solo trilogy (you can get 'em all from Ballantine Del Rey). Mr. Daley also scripted the 13-episode National Public Radio adaptation of *Star Wars*.